The Inn at the
Edge of the World

The Inn at the Edge of the World

Alice Thomas Ellis

A COMMON READER EDITION
THE AKADINE PRESS

The Inn at the Edge of the World

A Common Reader Edition published 1998
by The Akadine Press, Inc., by arrangement with the author.

A Common Reader Edition and fountain colophon are trademarks
of The Akadine Press, Inc.

ISBN 1-888173-45-9

2   4   6   8   10   9   7   5   3

For Stephanie

'It is not given to the Seal People to be ever content . . .
for their land — longings shall be sea — longings and
their sea — longings shall be land — longings.'

'The island mentality,' said Eric. He gazed out at the inn yard from where he sat in his tiny office, wondering what he had meant by this remark and why he had spoken aloud. Perhaps he was going mad.

'You've got a hangover,' said his wife. 'You always talk to yourself when you've got a hangover.'

Eric jumped. His wife walked about as silently as a house fly. She stood in the doorway, and to prove how cold she was feeling she clutched her cardigan across her chest with both hands. 'It's so sodding *cold*,' she said.

'I've lit the fire in the bar,' said Eric.

'Waste of money,' said his wife. 'There'll be nobody in.'

Not for the first time Eric tried to imagine how he'd feel if he murdered her. Not how he'd feel while he was doing it – the act, no doubt, would give him a momentary satisfaction – but how he would react afterwards. His principal emotion, he thought, would be embarrassment. Murder was neither respectable nor sophisticated; for the rest of his life he would feel miserable and shy if anyone so much as glanced at him. The whispers – '*He murdered his wife, you know.*' He had no real fear of the immediate consequences since he thought he would only spend a few years in jail with remission for good conduct. He could give a course on engineering to the other inmates. A number of wife-killers had got off very lightly recently. He had once asked a customer, a solicitor from Edinburgh, about the complexities of divorce. The man had advised against it these days. It was a lengthy, expensive and disruptive business, fraught with recrimination and ill-feeling. It was quicker and neater, he said, to murder your spouse, plead intolerable provocation or insanity, or what you would,

I

pay your debt to society and emerge from open prison to resume life with your property intact and no maintenance payments to worry about. Eric had been shocked, but as the solicitor had spent the day fishing and was presently warming himself up with a number of whiskies he had made allowances for him. The man could not be serious, for if he meant what he said he would endanger his own livelihood. It was popular wisdom that lawyers grew fat on the legal fruits of marital disharmony. Sometimes he reflected that an innkeeper convicted of murder might prove a draw to the morbid, but he had never cared for the limelight and did not relish the idea of himself as a sideshow. Besides, every now and then his wife still made him catch his breath. She had a way of looking up with a sudden smile that changed her face, changed the whole of her. At the moment she looked as sullen as a bull, bored and rather dangerous.

'So wear your fur coat, Mabel,' he said, spitefully. She loathed being called Mabel, and she had wanted a new fur coat for a long while. Once upon a time he had called her Ma Belle. Then, as he got more used to her, he had called her Maybe and sometimes Maybe Baby, until the time came when she had felt she knew him well enough to ask him not to do that; she preferred being called Poppet. Now, as a compromise, he usually called her Mab, but when she was being too awful he called her Mabel.

'What are you doing?' she asked. He tried to hide the paper he'd been typing on but she walked up behind him and took it from his hand. 'Dreading Christmas?' she read in an unnatural tone. 'Then get away from it all in a small hotel at the edge of the world . . .' Eric reached for the paper but she held it above her head. 'Oh, *honestly* . . .' she said.

'Why do you use that silly voice?' asked Eric.

'Because it's a silly advertisement,' said Mabel.

Eric lost his temper in a minor way. He pushed back his chair without considering the consequences, fetching her a

2

shrewd blow in the stomach as the arm-rest revolved. It was what is known as a captain's chair.

'Ouch,' said Mabel with an unjustifiable degree of outrage considering the circumstances. 'Can't you watch what you're doing, you ape?'

'I can't see out of the back of my head,' explained Eric, regaining self-control.

'If you ask me you can't see out of the front of your head,' said Mabel, fondling her diaphragm.

His control slipped again. 'Give that to me,' cried Eric, lunging forward to seize the paper.

Alarmed, Mabel shrank back. 'Don't you dare lay a finger on me,' she said. 'I told you that last time – you ever lay a finger on me again and . . .'

'That was an accident,' said Eric, weary now. 'You know perfectly well it was an accident.' A small barrel of beer had once rolled out of his hands in the inn yard and Mabel had put her foot under it. That was the way Eric saw it.

'Accident my foot,' said Mabel, unaware of the subtle resonance of this remark. 'You knew damn well I was there. I told you then – you ever lay another finger on me . . .'

It was guilt, thought Eric, that made her so determined to blame him for the occurrence. She had been particularly bad that day, taunting him as he had struggled all by himself to perform the multifarious tasks of a small innkeeper; asking him whether he was satisfied now that he had dragged her away from the comfort of their modern luxury home in Telford and dumped her here in the teeth of the Atlantic gales with no one to talk to and nowhere to go.

It was partly because of the people she had talked to and the places she went that Eric had resolved to realize a vague ambition and buy himself an inn at the edge of the world. It wasn't as though she had contented herself with talking to the sleek-suited sales executives who had thronged the lounge and patio of what the estate agent had described as their

3

detached luxury house, winter and summer; and it wasn't as though she had habitually gone to museums, theatres and picture galleries, back in what she referred to as 'civilization'. No, she had frequented dubious night spots, endangering her health, while claiming that she organized her social life only to further his career by mingling with influential people. The absurdity of this was such that he had never found words to refute it, and it was now quite possible that Mabel herself believed it to be so. He had left it too late to tell her she was talking crap, and had put himself in the wrong by bringing her away without due explanation. She thought him eccentric, unfeeling and irresponsible – completely lacking in sex appeal, in fact – and there was nothing whatever he could do about it.

'Well, I've warned you,' said his wife. 'You just touch me once more . . .' She dropped the paper on the desk, bored with it, and went off, moodily caressing her midriff.

Eric now hated his advertisement. He felt as exposed and shamed as if he had written a delicately secret poem about his soul and his wife had mocked it in the market place. He crumpled it up in his hand, walked across the narrow road to the sea's brink and threw it on the waves.

There was a grey seal out there. He watched it and thought it watched him back, head raised for a while from the waters that must surely, surely stretch to the world's edge.

As usual Eric felt less melancholy with the evening. If he was put to the torture he would never admit that he sometimes felt oppressed by the grey wastes of the ocean, the vastness of the sky with its set, cold stars. It was for these that he had left the smallness of the Midlands, the horrid comfort of modern houses where the bathrooms had no windows and begonias grew in boxes. He had come to find peace in the timeless spaces, but he wasn't making enough money and sometimes felt that he had been conned – as indeed he had

4

been. He had been deceived by the previous owner, who had given him an inaccurate estimate of the benefits accruing from the tourist trade and a wholly untrue assessment of the year's average profits. In a corner of his mind he knew this; had known it at the time, but declined to take it into account. He had wanted the pub too much to be put off by its disadvantages, and he didn't even resent the previous owner's dishonesty; it was only to be expected. What he did mind was the indifference of the land and sea about him, and if he had had the resolution to examine his feelings he would have found that he resented the way they ignored him. They just sat there. He might have been anyone. He had come prepared for a love affair with the sea and land, but his love was unrequited and now it was dying. Sometimes he felt afraid, for he was a rational man and rational men do not shrink from the loneliness of everything. Rational men do not acknowledge it, having more important matters to think about.

He closed the inner door of the bar against the wind from the sea, and went to kick the sparking log in the grate; the red-shaded lamps gave an illusion of warmth and his first two whiskies supplied the reality. Mabel was in her customary place at the bar. Not behind it, as he had naively expected she would be when they left Telford, but slumped on a stool, still clutching her cardigan about her with one hand and grasping a glass in the other. Since only her husband and the boatman were present she kept her skirt pulled well down over her knees to protect them from the draught.

The boatman spoke. 'Och,' he observed, 'there're no' many folks around for the time of the year.'

'Finlay,' said Eric, exasperated by this needless observation, 'it's October. Of course there're no' many folks around. The season's over.'

Finlay, who was a big Scotsman with a big Scots nose and a brow more geological than anatomical, went on talking. Usually the ingratiating native, when attempting to describe the customs of his country to an outsider, wears an expression that combines modest pride with self-deprecatory reservation, for while he may value his traditions and feel affection for them, he cannot believe that they truly hold much interest for the stranger, since strangers, by definition, have come from a wider, more sophisticated world – or so it is assumed by the innocent. Finlay did not wear this expression: Finlay appeared to regard the stranger with mildly amused contempt. He gave the impression that he knew what he knew and did not care in the least for the experience or opinions of the outsider – whatever they might be. As he got into his stride his accent became nigh impenetrable, but no matter: 'When Allan Maclean had the place,' he said, 'there were folks sleeping in heaps on the floor.'

'Why?' asked Mabel, in a better mood now that she too had had her first whiskies.

'Because all the bedrooms were full,' said Finlay.

'Why?' asked Eric in his turn. 'Why was the place full in October?'

'For the shooting,' said Finlay. 'For the game.'

'What game?' asked Eric, beginning to sense again the feeling of being somehow excluded, of not understanding. As far as he had been able to gather, it was at least two centuries since Allan Maclean had had the place.

'Why, the isle was wild with game,' said Finlay, who was doubtless exaggerating. 'With partridge, and capercaillies, pheasant and duck and deer.'

'I've never seen any,' said Mabel. 'All I ever see is poxy sea-gulls.'

'There're oyster catchers too,' said Eric defensively, 'and cormorants, and I've seen ducks.'

'What's happened to all this game then?' asked Mabel. 'I suppose they've shot it all.' Her tone was scornful, and Finlay gave her a brief impassive glance.

'Times change,' he said, unanswerably.

'We could restock it,' said Eric. 'Get some chicks from the mainland, a breeding pair of deer . . .'

Nobody took up this suggestion and the conversation died for a while until Eric's whiskies had restored his will to live. 'Finlay,' he said, 'if I get, say, half a dozen guests to stay over the Christmas period do you think your sister-in-law would come in and give me a hand?'

'Aye,' said Finlay, 'aye, she would.'

No one found this assurance on the lady's behalf surprising. Finlay's sister-in-law was out on almost constant loan, like a lawn-mower or a piece of farming equipment too valuable to be permanently owned by any one individual or organization. She was always available in a crisis, to rub the backs of the bedridden, watch the dying, mind those children whose mothers had gone off to Glasgow on the rampage, and help out in the inn – either behind the bar or behind the scenes, making beds and scones for tea and cleaning the rooms. Finlay made sure that her utility was well rewarded, for his sister-in-law lived with him and her sister, and he was responsible for her.

'Aye,' said Finlay again. 'Just let me know when you want her.'

'When the moon is made of green cheese, I should think,' said Mabel.

'I'm going to put an ad in some of the London weeklies,' explained Eric, whose courage was high again since night had flooded day, and the inn, all closed and sealed against the indifference of the wilderness, might have been a small boat bobbing through eternity, endlessly seaworthy. I obviously suffer from agoraphobia, thought Eric, but what he said was, 'We've all heard people moaning about Christmas, about how they're never going to go through another one, how they're going to find some small hotel at the end of the world and ignore the whole thing. Well, I'm going to give them the opportunity. There must be thousands of them out there.'

7

'You won't have room for them all,' said Mabel.

'I shall accept the first six,' said Eric with the calm dignity of the third whisky.

Mabel stared at the row of optics asking herself whether this deserved replying to. On the whole, she decided, it didn't: an argument of this type was always won by the person who could shout the loudest and, as she knew this would certainly be herself, it didn't seem worth the trouble.

A man who used to be a farmer came in from the dark for a pint. He had sold his livestock when the smallholding had proved uneconomic. Now he spent his time mending other people's tractors, catching lobsters in pots and encouraging visitors to the island to stay in the second-hand caravan he had installed in a disused field. Eric resented his enterprise since, as an incomer, he himself was not qualified to diversify his energies in the same fashion. He had an unexpressed sense that as long as he confined himself to running the inn he would be accepted, albeit somewhat reluctantly, but if he began to compete with the indigenous population by using his engineering skills or potting lobsters things untoward might begin to happen. He thought, with some indignation, that it was unfair for the islanders to offer accommodation to travellers who might otherwise have stayed at the inn in the way they were meant to, while denying him any opportunity to augment his income. It was, he supposed, something to do with the island mentality.

He wrote out his advertisement again that night, after closing time, and next day he posted it off to the various publications he considered fit to carry it.

'. . . inn at the edge of the world . . .' read Harry. He had read every word of the *Spectator*, starting as always at the back and going through like an Arab, from right to left. He had considered trying the competition and deferred the exercise. Now he was reading the small ads. The remains of his

8

breakfast – the shell of his egg, the crumbs of his toast and bitter marmalade, the dregs of his tea – he had meticulously disposed of, and had washed the dishes in cold water. He was a military man, disciplined and tidy, and he had been sad for almost as long as he could remember. In a moment he would put on his overcoat and go for his daily walk in Hyde Park: then, since it was Thursday, he would lunch at his club. Occasionally, or perhaps most days, he thought of death, but he was a Christian and had been a soldier and the option of suicide was not available to him.

His admiration for and envy of General Gordon who had died comparatively young, albeit in a possibly unenviable fashion – but then what mattered the means to so desirable an end – had led him to attempt an essay on the last days of Khartoum. The essay had grown and had stretched backwards to encompass all that he could discover about Charles George Gordon and now, to his surprise, he found he was well on the way to writing a book. He had never intended to do that, but he had realized that it was as good a way as any other to fill up the endless hours, and better than many. There was an emptiness inside him that once he had thought might be filled – by love or happiness or peace – but he had grown to understand that it could merely be lessened, contracted until the void ceased to exist, and he would be healed and whole. This, he knew, could only be fully accomplished with the assistance of the Grim Reaper, but writing helped a little.

He dreaded Christmas no more than any other time, and 'dread' was not the word for his response to life. It was more a weary astonishment at being confined in so seemingly purposeless an existence. His faith served only to illuminate and, to some extent, define his bewilderment: faith revealed the presence of a window opening to freedom, but the window was barred – faith itself forming the defining grille.

'Lord,' said Harry, as old and half-forgotten images of the island drifted through his head. Without knowing quite why he took paper and an envelope from his desk drawer and wrote off to Eric.

Jessica ate her breakfast on foot since she felt ridiculous sitting alone at the table with food in front of her. Eating on your own was absurd enough, she thought, without making a meal of it. She pulled a grapefruit into segments and spat the pith into the ashtray. One of the benefits of eating alone was that you could do that without being looked at askance by some man. Whenever Jessica thought of not living alone she thought of some man. At the moment she was enjoying being alone, but she wasn't certain how long this would last. Her principal fear at present was that she would get drunk and ask Mike to come back to her. Whatever the results of this were they would be disastrous. If he refused her pride would be shattered, and if he did come back the whole dreary business would start again. 'Yuk,' said Jessica. She opened the fridge and looked hopefully for a bottle of apple juice. There wasn't any, so she drank some milk from the carton. Then she wondered what to do next. She supposed she could always go and see her agent, who seemed to appreciate these small attentions. Jessica still could not get used to being greeted by agents with glad cries and welcome, since she remembered too well the times before she was successful when such people were always in meetings when she rang, or whisking out of sight through unmarked doors when she arrived in person at their offices. In the front office there had always been one of those all-purpose young girls so usual in publishing, publicity and public relations, and all liars. It was a bad world, thought Jessica censoriously, that taught all those indistinguishable young females to lie like that for a living. Still, it needn't bother her any more since she was famous now – well, fairly. She got large sums for appearing in or merely doing voice-overs for commercials and her agent loved her. She had also done well in film and television, but for some reason whenever she needed to reassure herself she thought of the vast sums she was paid for praising toilet soap and tea-bags. She supposed a person of more depth would be ashamed, or at least covertly deprecatory, of this activity, but it only gave her a sense of satisfaction, of universal acceptance. She was a household voice and a household face, if not a household word. The knowledge made her comfortable and it amused her. Mike had professed to despise the commercials, which was one of the reasons she had poured the coffee over him. He had then perversely accused her of being actressy. Only an actress, he had said, would do such a ludicrous thing: he said she was showing off. Jessica had found this irrational and infuriating, for surely any woman of spirit, be she waitress, wife or what-the-hell, would have done the same. It was then that she had decided they were incompatible, although she had to admit that it was Mike who had packed his bags and left. In leaving so hurriedly he had also left an assortment of his belongings. Every day Jessica debated with herself whether to send them round to him on a bike, thereby letting him see what she thought of him, or whether to wait for him to come and get them and see what he had to say for himself. It was a problem.

Outside, a paltry November rain was falling, which made the prospect of going out seem unattractive. On the other hand, what would she do if she stayed in? She was starting rehearsals of a play in the new year but that was some time away and she had nothing to do in the meantime except sometimes watch or listen to herself on TV (this had also maddened Mike). Her agent might find her something untaxing to do while she was waiting. She hated the waiting. She was afraid. She looked at herself in the glass over the fireplace and asked herself if she was that living cliché, an actress who felt unreal when she wasn't acting. No, she decided – for she had learned from that very profession that honesty was a prerequisite of performance – she was merely a woman who had been left by her lover. Why this should frighten her she didn't know: it might reasonably have made her angry or sad, but what she felt was fear. She percolated the coffee as she thought about it, for doing anything was better than doing nothing. If, she argued, Mike had been the cornerstone of her existence, then when he extracted himself it was only natural that her confidence, at the very least, should have been shaken – and confidence was her stock-in-trade – but it didn't feel like that: her confidence in her abilities was unimpaired. It was probably, she decided with dissatisfaction, that she was used to being half of a couple. Having been twice a wife and many times a mistress, she was unaccustomed to being single. It was some dreary atavistic residue that bedevilled her: a primitive instinct lingering on from the times when it was better that there were two of you, when it was convenient for one to go out hunting while the other picked nuts and berries and kept the baby from the ravages of the sabre-toothed tiger. But I haven't got a baby and there are no more tigers, she told herself. And the two of you would only have been part of a larger tribe, and I would deeply loathe being part of a tribe. Being part of a cast was different.

Jessica wearied of these reflections and started to read *Private Eye*, beginning with the Lonely Hearts column. It was by mere chance that, turning over the page, the word Christmas caught her eye and she read Eric's ad. For want of anything more constructive to do she ringed it round with her eyebrow pencil and went to put her clothes on. As she painted her face she realized she had blunted her eyebrow pencil by so misusing it, and was glad of the necessity of sharpening it, since that, too, was something to do. She took up her coat, put an arm in a sleeve and then took it off again. It was still raining after all, and she'd left her umbrella somewhere. She turned on the radio and heard the announcer heralding the morning service. She turned it off again, for on the other channels they would only be playing love songs.

Already her mantelpiece held several invitations to Christmas parties. The prospect made her feel slightly bilious and she resented their importunity. They had to be answered, and if she answered in the affirmative she'd have to turn up to them, and if in the negative she'd have to think of excuses, for her profession had also made Jessica meticulous in these matters. Offending people – be they her public or those concerned with management – could be harmful to the career. Her resentment increased until she took paper and an envelope from the cupboard under the telephone and wrote in answer to Eric's advertisement. There, she said to the pale-faced invitations, now I can't go to any of you. This gave her such satisfaction that she managed to get both arms into her coat and herself out of the front door on to the rainy street where she posted the letter. It took some time to find a cab, but she finally arrived at her agent's office.

'Jessica,' said the liar employed by her agent, 'you're soaked.' This was undeniably true.

'They didn't keep it in the fridge for long enough,' said Jessica, who always maintained an appearance of vivacity and originality in the presence of those underlings who were somehow concerned with her profession. 'If they'd frozen all those raindrops a bit more they'd have turned into snowflakes and I'd look lovely with them glittering in my hair.'

'You always look lovely,' said the liar, who hadn't really followed this flight of fancy. 'She's got someone in there at the moment but she won't be long.'

Jessica sat down with her copy of *Private Eye* and read the True Stories column, for the liar had started to type.

A door opened and she heard her agent's voice slightly raised. '. . . and if there're any more shenanigans, Jon,' she was saying, 'I won't be held responsible . . .'

A young man emerged through the door. 'I'll be *good*,' he said. 'Goodbye.' As he saw Jessica he said, '*Jessica*,' as though he were her best friend.

Her agent too cried, 'Jessica?' and Jessica, torn, contrived to throw a smile of glad recognition at the young man – who so far as she could tell she'd never seen before in her life – while hurrying to acknowledge and embrace her agent.

'Darling,' said her agent predictably, 'lovely to see someone sensible. Some *people* . . .'

'The beautiful young man?' asked Jessica compassionately, for she knew agents had a lot to put up with.

'He's a nightmare,' said her agent. 'I'm quite fond of him in a way, but he gets into scrapes and gets everyone's back up.'

Jessica couldn't have cared less, but she knew that agents have to express interest in all their clients initially in case some weird chance should shoot them to the top.

'But never mind him,' said the agent. 'How are you? I've been worried about you.'

This could only be because of Mike's defection since there had been no other untoward events in her life to give anyone cause for concern. At least she hoped there hadn't. The anxiety which is never far distant from the creative artist stirred briefly within her. Had a director spoken disparagingly of her? Had some management company vowed to have nothing more to do with her? She suppressed these doubts and said that her agent was sweet, but had no reason to alarm herself. One of the odder aspects of this way of life, she thought, was its very openness. Nobody had any secrets. Everybody in her world seemed immediately to know what everybody else was up to. In a way it was a relief, since while it was still necessary for one's pride's sake to put a good face on things there was no further need for dissembling.

'I won't pretend I don't miss him,' she said, for although in a way she didn't, she knew her agent wouldn't believe her, 'but it's rather wonderful to have the place to myself. Whenever he made a cup of tea he'd carry two teaspoons of sugar, from wherever the sugar bowl was to wherever his cup was. We had ants in the summer,' she added. It had occurred to her that the sugary trails were the probable reason for this. 'And . . .' she went on, 'he used to scratch his balls all the time.' This was another of the reasons she'd poured the coffee over him. As well as she knew him it would have somehow seemed indelicate to remonstrate openly with him about this habit.

'I can't stand that,' agreed her agent. 'It's almost worse than nose-picking.'

'He did that too,' said Jessica.

'You're well rid of him,' said her agent. 'Now, what can I do for you?'

'Nothing,' said Jessica. 'I was just passing.' Since she was out of her house her fear had vanished. She didn't mind waiting for the new year, and now she couldn't see why she should look for work when she didn't need the money. She thought she might possibly be suffering from a previously undiagnosed claustrophobia and determined that if it should overwhelm her again she would consult a psychiatrist. 'I'm going away for Christmas,' she said, 'so if I don't see you before I go I'll ring as soon as I get back.'

She said no more about going away and her agent asked no questions: she knew the movements of her clients not by interrogating them but by listening in on the grapevine. In the course of time she would know precisely how Jessica had spent Christmas. She was not particularly curious but she knew she'd find out.

As she left Jessica looked round for her copy of *Private Eye*, but it had gone. She reflected as she went off in search of another taxi that it was strange to be able to discuss with people the most intimate shortcomings of your paramour while feeling the need to conceal from them the fact that you were going to spend Christmas in a small hotel at the edge of the world.

★

When Jon strolled into his usual pub the usual customers at the bar sent up the usual groan. Jon, as usual, affected to take this as friendly badinage. He was of the opinion that his beauty and his personality were such that they could arouse only jealousy in others, but was sufficiently magnanimous to excuse them.

'Hi Jon,' said one, 'how are Kenny and Emma?'

Jon ignored this. 'Double brandy,' he said to the barman. 'I'm celebrating,' he said to no one in particular. He was pleased, not that Jessica had recognized him, for he would have expected no less, but because fortune had been so good as to throw them together again.

'Celebrating?' asked somebody else, sneering slightly while winking at his neighbour.

'Got a job,' said Jon. He didn't explain that this would entail hanging upside down outside a window while a deeper voice than his own extolled the virtues of a substance which, judiciously applied, would render the said window unearthly with brilliance. 'And I'm spending Christmas with Jessica,' he added. Until he spoke he had had no doubt that Jessica would be staying at the destination she had so determinedly ringed in black. Why else should Providence have left her copy of *Private Eye* for him to pick up? It was all meant, he knew. His horoscope had indicated some such happening and advised him to seize an opportunity.

Hearing himself speak he felt a moment's unease. Could there be any other reason why she had marked the advertisement? No, he decided, but just in case he added that the arrangements had to be finalized, taking no notice of the jeers that followed this amendment.

He left when he had drunk his brandy, having no fondness for the company of his fellows: they had heard what he had to say and so had served their purpose.

Anita surveyed her department with an unaccustomed sense

of dissatisfaction. It had extended, as was customary in the Christmas period, into the gardening section, which had been moved downstairs until such time as the hyacinths began to spring from their bulbs and the holly and tinsel were only a dusty memory. The encroachment had started in August which even Anita, dedicated as she was to the sale of stationery, considered too early, and the buyer had been travelling the world since April. The buyer was the actual source of Anita's present feeling of unease. She had not, considered Anita, quite achieved the right touch this season, having ordered from somewhere in the Far East a collection of rather soupily old-fashioned Christmas cards when the trend recently had been towards a more secular, jocular form of greeting. The shepherds, angels, wise men, pop-up camels, donkeys, fat-tailed sheep, etc. made her a little nauseous, reminding her of Sunday School, and she had gone so far as to argue with the buyer. 'In the Brent Cross branch,' the buyer had said, 'they can't get enough Mother and Childs.' Anita had been disposed to correct her grammar but had refrained. She was beginning to wonder if the buyer drank. It would not be surprising with all that foreign travel to manufacturers and trade fairs.

Over a modest lunch of quiche and salad in the staff canteen she read *The Lady* with concentration because she didn't feel like talking to anyone. When she came to the small ads the word 'Christmas' caught her eye. I hate Christmas she thought guiltily, surprising herself, and was about to turn back to an article on quail rearing when she saw the words 'the edge of the world'. She could get away from it all, she could go where there were no Christmas cards or Santa Clauses, no swanky buyer, nothing to remind her of work or the way that, in the end, Christmas itself always turned out to be a little disappointing. She'd never quite admitted that to herself before. She folded the magazine into her bag and when she got home to her empty flat she wrote to Eric to book a trouble-free Christmas. It was an act of defiance: she repudiated all the tinsel and glitter which had occupied the forefront of her mind for far too long, while all the work she had done had brought her insufficient credit.

Ronald was staring with wild incomprehension at the toaster, which was stubbornly refusing to relinquish the toast. It seemed to Ronald that if it could speak it would be saying something not only rebellious but disrespectful. The thing was bent on defying him, as indeed the dishwasher had been. The kitchen was littered with two-day-old dirty dishes; his bed was unmade and his clothes unwashed. Not merely had his wife left him but the cleaning lady had given notice. The two events, he suspected, were not unconnected. He wouldn't be surprised if his wife had bribed the cleaning lady to leave in order to spite him and make his life impossible. How was he to give his mind to his work when his home was in total disarray? The pain he felt at his wife's dereliction was rather less acute than his discomfort, the mute hostility of the toaster more wounding than his wife's recent coldness. In truth the cleaning lady had left when his wife left because she had worked for single gentlemen before and had found it too onerous. Lifelong bachelors were all right, domestically competent and orderly, but deserted husbands were far too much trouble. They left everything for her to do — their beds unmade, their clothes unwashed, and they wouldn't stack the dishwasher. Often they couldn't even control the toaster and expected her to gouge out the charcoal into which it had turned the bread, and make it better again.

'Bloody women,' said Ronald, wrenching out the electric plug from the wall. He was pleased with this decisive act. The words 'That'll show 'em' were manifest in his demeanour. It was nearly time for his first patient to arrive, and as his wife wasn't there to let her in he stood behind the curtain peering surreptitiously through the window. He had a theory that patients panicked if left too long with their finger on the bell. It made them feel rejected – a distressing sensation, as Ronald was learning to his cost.

Having dealt with and got rid of his first patient, he had ten minutes before the second arrived. Ten minutes to somehow get together a breakfast which would sustain him through the next fifty. He believed the transference process was disturbed when his stomach rumbled. Having abandoned all hope of toast he decided on bread and butter and a lightly boiled egg, but he had left the butter too long in the fridge and when he came to apply it to the bread he found he had cut the latter too thinly, so that it adhered in crumbs to lumps of the former. Never had he seen bread and butter like it. Ronald had been cared for by his mother until the day he married his wife and as a result he couldn't boil an egg. It was hard – both his egg and his circumstances were hard. His second patient noticed immediately he walked in that the doctor had a bit of dry egg yolk in his beard. It stayed on his mind throughout the session, seriously interfering with his free-associations. After fifty minutes it had lodged itself deeply in his subconscious and he was never quite the same again.

For lunch Ronald had cold baked beans, but only after a scene with the tin and the tin-opener that was attached to the wall. He had used an old-fashioned one in the end which his wife had kept in a drawer out of obscure sentiment, and which had rusted and gone blunt. As the time for dinner approached he became aware that he had spent the time with his last two female patients wondering, not about their various schizoid, paranoid and oedipal tendencies, but whether they could boil eggs. He was accustomed to wondering what the least unattractive female patients would be like in bed and had – more or less – rationalized and come to terms with it, but never before had his attention strayed in the direction of the kitchen. It was too bad. If his wife knew to what a pitch her desertion had brought him she would feel really dreadful. In believing this Ronald had gone beyond the bounds of what is customarily accepted as common sense, and had entered those arcane regions where only the concerned professional chooses to tread. At the portals of these regions – it is held by the psychiatric establishment – the man in the street, the patient, starts bucking and rearing and digging his heels in; for here in the unconscious are repressed all manner of matters he does not care to confront. Ronald, in his confused state, was telling himself that if his wife could be forced to realize the enormity of what she had done she would be cured and would return to him. It did not, of course, follow. Ronald was applying his discipline incorrectly, rather as a motor mechanic might imagine himself qualified to operate on a horse. What he was really telling himself was that if his wife had ceased to love him she must be insane.

Years of training analysis had made him into as competent a therapist as any, but, as is so often the case, it had done nothing to ease his own way through the troubled paths of human intercourse: rather it had made of him a single-minded, foraging creature intent on a goal imperceptible to others. His wife had perched, as it were, on a branch watching him uncomprehendingly as he sought through the thickets for a means by which he could form a perfect union with her. In the end she had simply grown fed up – not of waiting for him to achieve this union, for she was not conscious of desiring any such thing – but of watching and listening to his seemingly meaningless ramblings. She had found it all un-bearably boring, since she could never understand, not only what he was looking for, but what he was talking about.

Ronald's penultimate patient was a wealthy young woman, part heiress to a fortune based on sugar. He had harboured lustful fantasies about her for some time, but had denied himself too overt expression of these. Now, weakened by physical hunger, he found himself staring down at her as she lay, all mounds and curves, warm and well-nourished; and he wondered not only what she would look like without her clothes on, but what she was going to have for dinner. When she left he found himself following her down the steps and had to pretend he had merely gone out there to pick up the rubbish which had gathered around them. He stood in the dusk clutching a sheet of torn newspaper and a polystyrene box that had once contained a hamburger. When his patient had driven off in her BMW he put them down again on the pavement. He was starving. He was lonely. He had few friends, for most people regarded the members of his profession with the same suspicion they felt towards the tax inspector, the chief of police and, possibly, the vicar; and none of his fellow professionals liked each other much because of the internecine rivalry common in those spheres where conflicting, and often opposing, theories strive for dominance.

He was still standing, in a most unprofessional fashion, on the doorstep when his last patient arrived, a few minutes early.

'What's up, Doc?' inquired the patient, a brash and idle young man to whom Ronald had never warmed. Ronald declined to answer, but with stately tread led the way to the consulting room where for the umpteenth time he listened, bored stiff, as the young man, who actually appeared to enjoy these sessions, unreeled yet again a succession of memories, dreams and unseemly desires. When the fifty minutes were up, on the dot, Ronald cut him short, waited impatiently for the lad to write out his cheque for the meagre amount that was all he could afford until he found a job, and slammed the door behind him. If his wife persisted in staying away he would have to hire a receptionist which would be, considered Ronald, a ridiculous waste of money.

He went out for dinner, remembering just in time to carry a key so that he could get in again: his wife had always taken care of these details and he found he had to concentrate now on such trivia in order to save himself endless trouble.

Somebody – probably one of the better class of homeless who were proliferating under the government's economic strategy – had left a magazine between the bars of the railings, where doubtless he had leaned, reading, as he ate the remains of the hamburger which some richer person had abandoned in a litter bin.

Ronald took the magazine with him to the Indian restaurant round the corner where he ordered too many dishes because his wife wasn't there to prevent him. He glanced through the magazine without noticing which one it was until his eyes began to water as he injudiciously bit a chilli in half. Cooling down over a bowl of tinned lychees he read the small ads on the back page, where the word 'Christmas' leapt to his eyes. He hadn't thought about the coming festive season until now, and wondered whether the Indian restaurant would be open on Christmas day. Examining his feelings with clinical detachment he concluded that he was descending into an unacceptable degree of depression. This was confirmed when, on the way home, he first caught himself bending to look inside a closed car to see if it contained his wife, and then found he had walked down a side street after a woman who vaguely resembled her.

Sitting on the edge of his unmade bed, staring at the wallpaper, he noticed the magazine lying on top of his overcoat on the floor. Carefully this time he read the ad which had mentioned Christmas. If he had to live through Christmas alone he would do it in the small hotel at the edge of the world, for he was beginning to fear that if he continued in this frame of mind he would commit some impropriety towards a female and well-fed patient which would lead to his being struck off. So strongly did he feel that when the morning came he telephoned Eric to book his room.

'Well, that's seven,' said Eric, concealing his satisfaction with a casual frown as he made a note of Ronald's name.

'Seven what?' asked Mabel who, naturally, knew perfectly well. She was eating a sardine sandwich and reached out with a greasy grasp for her husband's list. He looked away from her hand and began to note down what supplies he might need from the mainland. 'They sound a dreary lot,' observed Mabel.

'How can you tell?' asked Eric, who was feeling sufficiently relaxed to find this diverting rather than merely childishly annoying.

'The Chinese have an idea that you can tell everything about a person by their name,' said Mabel, beguiled by his mild tone into making explanations where she had originally intended only to wound. Then she wished she had thought of some other explanation as Eric smiled. A person called Mabel, she reflected bitterly, could not really afford to be superior about other people's names. 'I thought you were only taking six,' she said.

'I've taken seven,' said Eric, 'because somebody might drop out.'

Mabel thought it entirely likely that they would all drop out. She had never liked the island from the moment she set foot on it, and as the months went by she had begun to hate it with a wild and spiteful passion. She perceived it as nothing but a trap, and she felt like a creature going round and round in desperate circles, powerless and stupid. She could feel herself getting stupider and stupider as each day passed, and she could think only of her imprisonment, forgetting all that had gone before. She hardly bothered to try and remember what life had been like – the freedom, the gaiety, the long nights, the laughter, the men – and was only aware of the dark hill, the narrow shores and the endless moaning of the sea. It made her think of things she did not want to think about: of sorrow and loss. The whole island seemed to her implicit with loss, a symbol of deprivation and grief; but when she complained she spoke only of the cold, the boredom, the lack of modern facilities and the absence of companionship. As a result Eric found her increasingly shallow and trivial. Much of the time he could not remember the girl she had been. At first he had said, 'I only bought this place for you. I thought you'd be happy here,' which was not completely true, nor yet completely false. (At his first sight of her she had been rising from the water, the impossibly blue water of a municipal swimming pool, her grey eyes wide and bright as she blinked away the chlorine, her dark hair smoothed short and close to her skull.)

Eric had said as she moped and whined, 'You can swim as much as you like. You've got all the sea to swim in now,' and she would say in the apathetic voice of a beaten child, 'I don't want to swim in the sea.' Eric had often wanted to strangle her for her perversity: he had seen joy in that girl in the water.

Sometimes Mabel dreamed of the sea, but when she woke she thought only of the channel between the island and the mainland.

She hummed to herself, a broken, drifting tune of things half-forgotten. 'What if they all come?' she asked, cutting short her melody.

'I'll clear out the far room at the end of the passage, just in case,' said Eric. 'I'll take one of the single beds from one of the front rooms, and there's that spare chest of drawers on the landing. No problem.'

'How fascinating,' said Mabel, idly pushing down a cuticle.

'I'll get Finlay's sister-in-law to help me,' said Eric.

'You do that,' said Mabel.

The room at the end of the passage made Eric think of an orphanage, or perhaps a lunatic asylum, full as it was of unwanted things, or things that had lost their purpose. Most of them had been abandoned by the previous owner and some of them seemed to have been constructed by someone whose mind was wandering at the time. What, for instance, was the conical object formed of pink, quilted plastic? Somebody must have found himself in possession of a piece of pink quilted plastic and made it into a cone. But why? Eric lifted it from the stained divan on which it reposed and trod on it, but its maker had given it a substructure of steel and he merely dented the plastic. Finlay's sister-in-law silently forced it into a bin liner. 'What the devil is it?' asked Eric petulantly. She shrugged and pushed an old pillow in on top of it. Eric didn't protest. The pillow, like nearly everything else in here, was too far gone to be salvageable. 'I'll make a bonfire in the yard,' he said, breaking some strips of plywood over his knee.

They cleared out piles of old magazines, a broken umbrella, a seatless push-chair, a lidless tin trunk with a dead mouse in it and a chiffonier which Eric hacked to bits *in situ*. The dust occasioned by all this energy made him sneeze.

'Ach,' said Finlay's sister-in-law, who was a woman of few words.

The room now contained only a wardrobe and an ottoman. Eric opened both. All that the wardrobe held was a hat-box which must have dated from the turn of the century and which Eric decided to keep, and in the ottoman was a moth-eaten coat of a thin, dark fur. For a moment he thought it was his wife's and wondered how it had got there, but then he saw that it was far more dilapidated than hers and he put it in the bin liner. Finlay's sister-in-law took it out again. Again Eric did not protest. If she wanted it she was welcome to it.

There were a few old off-white sweaters on a shelf in the top of the wardrobe. Eric took them down and considered them: he could feel Finlay's sister-in-law watching him and wondered whether she wanted them too. He couldn't be bothered to ask. They still seemed quite serviceable and not too full of holes, oily and harsh to the touch though they were. As he held them they felt unlike ordinary clothes; not soft and biddable, designed to keep the wearer warm, but as though they had a shape and purpose of their own, unconnected with ordinary human everyday needs. He put them back on the shelf. 'Uncomfortable things,' he observed, and closed the wardrobe door.

He took all that was combustible down to the yard and made it into a neat pile, while Finlay's sister-in-law dampened down the dust by squirting it with water from a plastic bottle. Then she swept it up and washed down the door and the window-frames and the skirting-board until the room was perfectly clean.

Eric, coming back to collect his jacket, for it was cold in the darkening yard, commended its cleanliness while deploring the decorative condition revealed by its bareness.

'I'll paint the walls and ceiling,' he said. 'It won't take me five minutes now we've got it clear.'

Finlay's sister-in-law didn't care what he did with it, although she didn't say so. She had performed her task and now she was going home.

Eric took a can of rancid vegetable oil from the shelf where the previous owner had left it and poured it over his bonfire, appreciating the enforced economy of this move. He lit it from below with a match and the flames took hold. Smoke began to rise and, belatedly, he licked his finger and held it aloft to test the direction of the wind. Mabel would remark on it if the smoke flooded the inn. Happily, if somewhat incomprehensibly, since by the evidence of Eric's finger the wind was coming inwards, it drifted out towards the sea.

It seemed another instance of his failure to understand the natural rules that governed this inscrutable island, but he wasn't going to brood about it now. He stood, using the yard broom as a goad when the flame faltered, watching the sparks sail up on the smoke.

There was a figure walking down the narrow road that held the shore back from the inn. 'Damn,' said Eric, for if this was a customer there was no one in the bar to serve him.

The figure as it came level revealed itself as a boy carrying a fishing rod. Then the smoke thickened in a sudden gust and he was obscured. Eric thought he saw him lift a hand in greeting, but when the smoke cleared he had gone.

Next day Eric painted the far room with a can of emulsion paint the previous owner had left in the shed. It was a fleshy shade which Eric would not have chosen himself, but beggars, he said, *could* not be choosers. Anyway in the end it made no odds because one guest rang to say she couldn't make it after all, and another simply didn't turn up. Eric vowed that in future he would demand a deposit, but he was rather relieved.

There were only five guests for Christmas.

Jessica and Harry sat opposite each other across a white-topped table in a first-class compartment on the London-to-Glasgow Express. Harry, having been an officer, had always travelled first class, and now that Jessica was quite rich and famous she too had grown accustomed to this habit. Anita was travelling second class, further down the train in a non-smoking area. Ronald was also travelling in second-class accommodation because his wife's desertion had left him unconfident and fearful that he might, at any moment, find himself penniless. He rationalized his decision by telling himself that, these days, there was very little difference between first and second class. He was right, but he was, nevertheless, slipping unawares into an unfortunate trend towards self-deception.

Jessica had bought a Penguin copy of *The Tenant of Wildfell Hall*, thinking she might as well improve her mind on this long journey. She had read very little except for Shakespeare, Shaw, Ibsen, Ayckbourn, etc. and hence, while in some ways she could appear erudite, in others she was in danger of seeming a perfect fool.

She had been reading for some time with increasing incredulity. As the train neared the Lake District she flung the book from her on to the table with a cry of 'Oh *no!*'

Harry smiled inquiringly as to the reason behind her histrionic gesture. While as yet they were unaware that they shared a destination, each had been covertly observing the other with quiet approval, assuming that they were the same sort of human being. They looked alike. Harry was handsome with clear eyes and white hair, and Jessica had a large pleasant face, which she could, when called upon, make beautiful. This is the most useful sort of face for an actress.

'Have you read this?' she demanded, indicating her book.

Harry picked it up and looked at it. 'No,' he said, 'I'm afraid I haven't.'

'Don't be afraid,' said Jessica. 'It's terrible. The heroine is terrible.' The train sped through as she spoke. 'Listen,' she said, opening the book at random. 'Now, she's been playing the piano. This is her: "I was exerting myself to sing and play for the amusement, and at the request, of my aunt and Millicent, before the gentlemen came into the drawing-room (Miss Wilmot never likes to waste her musical efforts on ladies' ears alone): Millicent had asked for a little Scotch song, and I was just in the middle of it when they entered." Now, Mr Huntingdon, who she's got her eye on, asks Miss Wilmot to play, so Helen hops up from the piano in a huff. Listen. "I had quitted it immediately upon hearing his petition. Had I been endowed with a proper degree of self-possession, I should have turned to the lady myself, and cheerfully joined my entreaties to his; whereby I should have disappointed his expectations, if the affront had been purposely given, or made him sensible of the wrong, if it had only arisen from thought-lessness; but I felt it too deeply to do anything but rise from the music stool, and throw myself back on the sofa, suppressing with difficulty the audible expression of the bitterness I felt within. I knew Anabella's musical talents were superior to mine, but that was no reason why I should be treated as a perfect nonentity. The time and the manner of his asking her appeared like a gratuitous insult to me; and I could have wept with vexation." She reminds me of somebody,' added Jessica thoughtfully. 'Who does she remind me of?'

'Mr Pooter,' said Harry.

'Yes, of *course*,' said Jessica. 'You are clever.' She had listened to one of her friends reading *The Diary of a Nobody* on the radio.

A traveller at an adjacent table was puzzled by this exchange. She had watched Harry and Jessica get on the train separately, and they hadn't said a word to each other until now. Yet they obviously knew each other well. She had been wondering why Jessica looked so familiar, but gave up racking her memory in order to speculate on their relationship. Father and daughter? Husband and second wife? No, she didn't think they were married. They were smiling at each other too openly. She concluded, not being a person of great imagination or depth of perception, that Harry was the managing director of an international company, and Jessica was his personal assistant. They were probably travelling to a conference to be held at Gleneagles over the Christmas period.

'Aah,' said Jessica. 'Tears are rising unbidden to her eyes and she's burying her head in the sofa cushions that they might flow unseen. What a *creep*.'

'Would you like to read the *Spectator*?' offered Harry.

'Thank you,' said Jessica. 'Would you like a Polo mint?'

At this evidence of a new friendship being formed the fellow traveller grew confused again. She made up her mind that the managing director had only just engaged his personal assistant and they were feeling their way as they got to know each other even better.

After a while they went together to the bar and when they returned the fellow traveller was completely thrown, for they had discovered that they were both going to the island and their relationship had changed. Jessica was always excited and animated by coincidence and Harry was surprised and quietly gratified to have found an undemanding and congenial companion. He had intended to spend his island time alone as far as that was possible, lost in thought in streaming coves and rocky embrasures, and if there were other guests he had expected that he would find himself under the necessity of avoiding them. He had not thought that he might make a friend.

Anita had sworn not to give a single thought to work for a whole week. She stared out of the window at the unprepossessing scenery and wondered what her fellow guests would be like. It had not occurred to her, as it had to Harry, that there might not be any. A passing conifer plantation reminded her again of her department. She hoped the under-section manager was coping well, but not too well; she didn't like to feel she wouldn't be missed. She was picturing the shelves of executive toys and wondering how they were selling when she remembered she wasn't going to think about work, and stared resolutely at a field and some sheep. She worried a little that they might be feeling cold and hoped she had brought enough woollies to keep herself warm. It was probably always warm in Taiwan where the buyer had spent a week earlier in the year, purchasing a large consignment of Christmas tree fairies with slanting eyes. The buyer had justified her choice with rather too much conviction and Anita was certain that she had bought them after lunch when her judgement was impaired. Anita couldn't really see why she should have fairies in her department anyway: paper plates, cups and serviettes perhaps, even jigsaw puzzles didn't seem too out of place, but baubles and fairies could surely have been displayed elsewhere, and she couldn't see any justification at all for having a rack of Santa Claus suits situated to the left of the Advent calendars. It was hard being titular head of a department and yet at the mercy of another's whims.

Rain began falling on the already damp countryside, and

she asked herself why she hadn't taken a package trip to Florida. The reason was that she had thought it more chic to go to a small hotel at the edge of the world. Exotic foreign travel was becoming curiously vulgar: everyone was doing it either for pleasure or business. It was more elegant to be travelling to a small island; the cold and the wet an added distinction, for it must be evident to everybody that if people were prepared to put up with these conditions the experience must be richly, if subtly, rewarding. It was far more *tasteful*, thought Anita with uncharacteristic defiance. So there.

'They'll drown,' said Mabel happily. 'They'll all be sick as dogs and perishing cold and then that rotten old boat will sink and they'll all drown. Still, you'll have their deposits.'

Eric took no notice of her, not mentioning that he had not demanded deposits since that would draw upon him her awful scorn. He had decided one evening that it would make an interesting start to the holidays for his guests to sail over, not on the McBrayne ferry, but in Finlay's boat. Finlay, not surprisingly, since Eric paid him well for these services, had agreed with him.

'It's a rusty old tub and they'll get their clothes filthy,' Mabel went on, 'and it doesn't half rock – even when the sea's as flat as a mill pond.'

'You've been across in it when you couldn't get on the ferry,' said Eric.

'That's how I know what it's like,' said Mabel, 'only I'm not fussy.'

Eric didn't say anything to this because he couldn't think of anything.

'It's not seaworthy,' said Mabel. 'Not really.'

'Yes it is,' said Eric.

'Tisn't,' said Mabel.

Finlay seemed unconcerned by this clash of opinion: he was dressed in sou'wester and sea-boots, and Eric was almost

31

certain he had dressed the part deliberately. He was glad someone was entering into the spirit of the thing. 'Radio working now?' he asked. There had been some flaw in this useful piece of equipment.

'Aye,' said Finlay.

'That's lucky,' said Mabel.

'Have you got the flares?' asked Eric.

'Aye,' said Finlay.

'And you'd better take a couple of duffel coats from here in case anyone's cold,' said Eric, who was beginning to wonder whether there might not be something in what his wife was saying. It was a grey day with a hint of mist.

'Aye,' said Finlay.

'And you'd better get going,' said Eric, adding hastily in order to prevent Finlay from saying 'Aye' again, for it was getting on his nerves, 'You don't want to keep them waiting on the quay.'

When Finlay had gone Eric went to take a final look at the rooms which he and Finlay's sister-in-law had prepared. The previous owner had had a regrettable passion for stripes. The wallpaper, curtains and counterpanes had all been resolutely striped and several chairs had had tartan-covered cushions on them. Eric had removed all these in his first enthusiasm and replaced them with a pale and restrained chintz he had got cheap when a shop in Glasgow, which had been too-pale and restrained for its own good, went out of business. On the floors were Indian rag rugs which he had bought from a market-stall, and, as a little joke, he had hung some pictures of *Highland Kine* and the *Stag at Bay* on the walls. He'd got them from another market-stall late in the afternoon when the stall-holder was thinking only of getting home, out of the puddles. They had been a bargain even though no one else had wanted them. Mabel hadn't seen the joke. She'd said *'Honestly'* and laughed for the wrong reason. Now she was walking behind him, getting in the way whenever he turned and irritating him by humming a song about a small hotel and a wishing-well.

'Can't you find something to do?'

'What?' inquired Mabel. 'What is there to do here?' She was developing one of her worst moods, and Eric wondered fretfully how she was going to behave when the guests arrived. She could be indescribably offensive when she put her mind to it.

'If you're going to be like that,' he said, 'I don't know why you don't go and stay with your mates in Glasgow.'

She had met her mates from Glasgow when they were taking their summer break on the island and driven Eric nearly out of his mind by giving them free drinks when he wasn't looking, and often when he was. He had heard that they lived in some style on the dole, pursuing an idle and carefree way of life and playing borrowed musical instruments for their own satisfaction.

'I might,' she said. 'I might just do that.'

Eric was painfully torn. He could hardly bear to imagine what she got up to when she was away from him, but he dreaded the prospect of what she might do if she stayed. Perhaps, he thought, if she did something really outrageous and really ruined his business, he could finally stop loving her. In the end that would be best.

'You've left it a bit late,' he said. 'There'll be no more ferries running after today. How'll you get there?'

'Oh,' said Mabel. 'Oho, I'll get there. You just watch me.'

'Walk, will you?' said Eric. 'Swim?'

She was moving away from him towards the stairs, and as he spoke she stopped, turned and slapped him on the ear. She'd never done that before. Eric was stunned and then angry. He slapped her back. He'd never done that before.

'Right,' said Mabel before she grew incoherent. 'That does it. That's the third time. I told you before, you touch me once more . . .' Then she grew incoherent.

33

Finlay's sister-in-law, down in the kitchen, heard the screaming and shook her head over the loin chops she was defrosting under the tap.

Eric wanted to say '. . . you started it . . .' but he didn't get the chance. His wife was beside herself.

The four who had been on the train stood on the quayside amid the wasteland while a few gulls swooped, grieving, over their heads.

'Oh crikey,' said Jessica. They had been carried here from Glasgow Central on another, smaller train and thus been spared the peculiarly unpleasant aspects of the town which lay behind the docks, to all appearances deserted and as derelict as a collection of concrete bunkers can be. It was similar to the less salubrious parts of Calais although not as large, and the dock area itself offered nothing to ease the eye. There wasn't a ship in sight.

'No rigging,' said Jessica, disconsolately.

Since the four of them had gathered on the spot where Eric's letter had directed them, to the right of the place assigned to the roll-on-roll-off ferry, she spoke again. 'Are we all going to the edge of the world?' she asked.

'Well yes,' and 'Yes,' said Ronald and Anita.

'I think we got there,' said Jessica since she couldn't see the horizon which had disappeared under the mist. 'Where, I ask myself, is the much-vaunted local boatman?'

'He'll be along,' said Harry, who had never panicked.

'What if he doesn't?' said Jessica. 'What if he doesn't come at all? What if the craft has foundered and he's gone down to Davy Jones's locker? Oh crikey.'

'Then we'll take a cab back to Glasgow and put up there for the night,' said Harry. 'But he'll be here. Wait and see.'

Anita was grateful for Jessica's show of nerves. The circumstances called for something like that, and Jessica had saved

34

her the necessity of doing it herself and going too far. Jessica, she considered, had done it well: she had voiced the misgivings of all of them and expressed their doubts succinctly and clearly. Now it was out in the open.

In fact, Jessica was very tired and growing very cold. She wanted only to get somewhere warm with a stiff drink to hand and she no longer cared where it was. 'He's *late*,' she said.

Finlay was late because Mabel had made him come back and get her. Her voice had reached him over the ether and he had turned round and come back for her. She had thrown the things she needed – the most remarkable of which were a PVC bustier and knickers – into a hold-all and had fled the hotel.

'Listen,' said Harry. 'He's coming now.'

The wind was rising and it was beginning to grow dark when the reassuring figure of Finlay came moving towards them out of the sea spray. The practical and nautical impression he gave was marred by the woman who followed him, staggering on high heels and swearing. As she came level she addressed them. 'You're effing mad,' she said. 'You know that? You're all effing mad,' and she staggered swiftly on, dragging her hold-all, clad only in a miniskirt and a short black jacket with very wide shoulders.

'Ye should have brought your coat,' called Finlay after her, and 'How will ye get to Glasgae?'

No answer came. Mabel was going to hitch-hike to Glasgow. She wasn't afraid of being murdered because a stranger could never summon up enough feeling to murder a person in her overwhelmingly passionate frame of mind: she was in no mood to be victimized.

Finlay turned to those who were about to sail with him. 'There're only four of ye,' he said, as though it was their fault.

'Oh God,' said Jessica wearily. 'You mean . . .?'

'We'll bide a wee,' said Finlay.

Jessica peered at him suspiciously, wondering if the hotel had hired a professional Caledonian rustic without any knowledge of navigation or the way of the tides. He reminded her of a lay-figure outside a fishmonger's in his sou'wester, oilskins and boots, or a bit-part actor likely to ruin a production by trying to upstage the principals.

Jon came running lightly across the quay. 'Am I late?' he asked. 'I flew.' He bent and kissed Jessica on the cheek, surprising her slightly, for still, as far as she knew, she'd never seen him before in her life. However, she was getting used to being greeted by strangers so she made no remark.

'When you say you flew,' said Ronald, who until now had been more or less silent, 'do you mean that you hurried or that you came in an aeroplane?'

Jon stared at him. 'I took the plane,' he said. 'It saves hours.'

'You were still late,' said Ronald, picking up his case and looking expectantly at Finlay.

'Aye,' said Finlay, leading the way to the boat.

Jessica caught a last sight of the woman in high heels teetering towards civilization. 'Who do you suppose that was?' she said to Harry. 'Was she a local, do you imagine? Are they all like that?'

'No,' said Harry, 'they won't all be like that.'

'I do hope so,' said Jessica, 'because really I came to get away from it all.'

She regretted saying this since it sounded not inappropriate to Helen Huntingdon of Wildfell Hall, but there was no time to expatiate as Finlay was taking their luggage from their hands and stowing it in the hold. At least that's where she assumed he was putting it, calling on memories of nightmare childish experiences, sailing with her family when not only their personalities but their vocabulary underwent a bewildering transformation. She supposed it was what was meant by a sea-change. She chose precisely the right moment to step aboard Finlay's boat: that is, when it had bobbed close to the pier. She had seen too many people dithering about the decision, leaving their leap until the boat had bobbed away again and thus losing their footing, their shoe and, sometimes, doubtless, their lives down in the narrow deeps between ship and sea wall.

Anita dithered, but Finlay held her fast in a strong, slightly fishy, oilskin-clad arm. They went into the cabin and Jessica's spirits fell with the descent. The high-heeled woman in the bad temper had reminded her of some of her friends who seemed to believe that unless they were feeling something very deeply they were not alive. Until perhaps this moment she had been inclined to believe it herself, but weariness and the constraint of the cabin full of people made her yearn for peace and space – for what she had thought she was coming to. A mirage, a dream, thought Jessica disenchantedly, realizing as she reflected that the cabin actually held only three people, since Harry and Jon were out on deck. As there were only three of them, in a short time they would have to start talking to each other. Five people can sit in silence, smiling occasionally as they meet each other's eyes, but three must converse or an awkward and anti-social atmosphere results. Jessica said something about fresh air and also went up on deck. Jon was standing with one foot on the rail, the wind in his golden hair. Get a load of Fletcher Christian, thought Jessica. His nose would soon turn bright red for it was too cold out there to be playing a part.

Harry was standing by Finlay, who was gazing ahead as he guided his boat to the island. Jessica heard Finlay say, 'So you've come back then.' And she heard Harry say, 'Aye, I've come back.' That, she thought, could have been intriguing if she wasn't so tired, for Harry had not told her that he'd been here before.

★

Eric's hand trembled as he stirred the blue-sparking driftwood in the fireplace. He was no longer angry. He had only been angry for a second and his brief rage had not been enough to arm him against his wife's torrential fury. He had faced an elemental, hostile force and now was feeling, not only inadequate but wounded: all his certainties displaced. Where am I? he wondered as he trembled. What's going on? He had done nothing to deserve such an onslaught, he didn't understand anything, and how was he to face his imminent guests, feeling as he did? He was half tempted to jump in the sea or, less drastically, jump in the hotel van and drive to the cliff top where he could cower alone under an old tarpaulin and not have to talk to anyone until the trembling stopped. It was surely unnatural to feel as shaken as he did. Unmanly, thought Eric as he poured himself a whisky, but it wasn't his pride that was hurt. He'd been frightened. Now he was frightened that Mabel would never come back, and equally frightened that she would, and he wished he could put a name to the emotions he was experiencing: it would make them more tolerable.

It was nearly dark in the yard when he went out to collect more logs than he actually needed for the night. He looked seawards for the lights of Finlay's returning boat and saw someone else looking seawards, standing on the edge of the shore; standing still in the wind and the cold.

'What's he waiting for?' said Eric to himself, aloud. He was fairly sure it was the boy he'd seen the other night, but he didn't hail him as he might have done if he had felt normal. Curiosity had gone temporarily to ground together with courage, and Eric was conserving whatever shreds of sociability he had left to gratify his guests.

Thank God for Finlay's sister-in-law. The inn was clean and tidy, swept and garnished, the bar room fire high and bright. Eric began to feel better as he looked into the kitchen. Perhaps he should have married Finlay's sister-in-law, except that, competent as she was, she was a bit odd. She never said anything. On the other hand, reflected Eric, Mabel, too, was more than a bit odd and she said too much: she wasn't unlike Finlay's sister-in-law to look at when you came to think of it, only she dressed differently. The woman wiping down the kitchen table was wearing a brown Crimplene dress under a flowered apron – yet they had the same grey eyes and smooth dark hair. Eric found himself close to Finlay's sister-in-law before he remembered himself and went to wash his hands in the small basin that the council had made him install for hygienic reasons. The previous owner had never bothered with such refinements, which annoyed Eric when he hadn't got too much on his mind to worry over trivia; it aggravated the mild paranoia habitual to newcomers to an island community.

The inn door creaked, signalling an arrival, and Eric went reluctantly to the hall, wondering which stereotype of mine host he could assume in time: he knew of several, ranging from the hearty to the sardonic, but he didn't now feel sufficiently confident to carry off any of them. He didn't need to, as it happened. Not immediately.

'Oh, hallo, Professor,' he said without enthusiasm. It was only one of those incomers who had bought a house on the island for the purposes of holidaying there: a mean man in Eric's view, who drank alcohol-free lager with lime and not too much of that. There was a girl with him wearing the guarded, faintly sulky air of a girl who is not too stupid to know that she is the latest in a series of similar girls. Eric had noticed, over the months, that several incomers had bought houses on the island apparently for the sole purpose of conducting clandestine affairs. The professor kept an old duffel coat which he made all his women wear, probably so that he would recognize them if his memory slipped.

'Hallo, Isabel,' said Eric.

The girl did not respond.

'Sophie?' he ventured.

39

Silence.

'Agnes . . .?' Oh *shit*, he might have learned to keep his mouth shut by now. He would have done if he hadn't been so discomposed.

'This is Jennifer,' said the professor cheerfully.

'What'll you have?' asked Eric, slipping behind the bar. 'Down here for long?'

'Two halves of lager, alcohol-free, with lime,' said the professor. 'Just till the New Year.'

He sat on a bar stool and began to ask questions to prove that he was conversant with island ways and the inhabitants. Eric polished a glass and wished he'd go. Those locals who did frequent the inn were wont to melt away when they saw the professor. The girl stood, restively twisting her glass. Poor cow, thought Eric, without compassion. The door opened and he looked up, hopeful now, but it was yet another incomer. 'Evening, Mrs H.,' he said. This was the female of the species. When her husband was away on business she brought men with her to her white house on the hill. 'How's Graham?' he inquired nastily, for he happened to remember that her husband was called John.

'He's fine,' she said without turning a hair.

No shame, thought Eric. None of them had any shame. They treated the island like a brothel. He looked back to the time when he had pictured his bar full of local characters gathered for the edification and amusement of the gently bred guests who had just unpacked their pigskin suitcases in the charming ambience of their bedrooms before coming down, talking animatedly among themselves, to drink a lot of expensive liquor before dining, while his wife chirruped and shone like a budgerigar in crisp cottons, scent and fresh lipstick. His ideas of marriage and the typical hostelry were hopelessly out of date. Mrs H. ordered a mineral water with ice and a slice of lemon.

★

Finlay tied up his boat and helped his passengers ashore by way of the amateurish pier which the locals begrudgingly held together, each hoping that somebody else would do something to make it more stable, and if not that the council might. There was enough light from the lamp hanging outside the inn to show them where they'd be when they got there, but not enough for them to see where they were going. Consequently they shuffled along the narrow shore road, carrying their luggage and wondering what they'd let themselves in for. It was beginning to rain.

Hearing the sound of a number of people putting down their bags, Eric went into the hall. Seeing through the open door that rain was sifting through the lamplight he felt guilty. They were here for Christmas after all. 'That'll turn to snow by the morning,' he said. 'Now I'll show you to your rooms and then perhaps after you've signed in you'd like a drink before dinner . . . on the house,' he added, as he noticed their downcast mien, and he wondered whether he should have met them at the pier with the van, even though it was only a hundred yards or so. He had a moment of terror as he realized that he was solely and personally responsible for keeping these people contented for the length of their stay. Maybe he should have listened to Mabel. Oh, Mabel . . .

One by one they gathered in the bar.

Anita and Jessica had both changed their clothes for the evening: Anita because she'd been well brought up, and Jessica because the bottoms of her trousers had got splashed walking from the boat. She had a lot of fashionable clothes that she had gathered, in one way or another, from kindly wardrobe mistresses who seemed to know what would suit her better than she knew herself. It saved a lot of trouble and thought, but she always felt guilty when she dirtied them.

Eric was delighted with these ladies: already they had

41

added tone to his establishment. He felt quite recovered and able to handle the responsibilities of the landlord; and now he thanked God that Mabel had gone. No longer need he worry that she would shock, alienate or sleep with any of the guests. As he regarded Jon his thankfulness increased. Mabel would have had him for breakfast. It was also fortunate that the guests were all single, since he usually had trouble with married couples. Men, who would not if left to themselves complain, were often impelled by the presence of their wives to mention that the soup was a little cold, the cup cracked or the steak tough; while the women could be worse, tracking him through the hotel to tell him, tight-lipped, that the creaking of the inn sign had kept their husband awake all night and with the pressure of work he'd been under he needed all the sleep he could get and they'd come here to rest didn't he realize. Sometimes they complained that the waitress had insulted their husband, and as, at one time, he had employed casual labour from the mainland, Eric had to admit that they were probably right. There had been an incident in the summer when Mabel's Glaswegian mates were making merry and a wife had come down in her nightie, beckoned him from the bar and abused him in front of everyone. She hadn't tackled the mates. Oh no. They were wearing black leather, and some of them, male and female, had their bald heads tattooed. What, Eric had wondered, did she expect him to do? He was running a business, wasn't he, an inn? People came to inns to drink, didn't they? It was bad luck if the interests of the residents and the passing trade proved to be incompatible, but what was he supposed to *do* about it? It was also exasperating to observe, when these married couples were together, that they didn't seem unduly devoted to each other, eating in silence unless one of them found something untoward in the salad. Eric had not, himself, been married long enough to appreciate the nuances of the married state.

Sometimes, still, he pictured himself throwing out the mates in ones and twos to lie in the seaweed, but it would have been impracticable to try. He hoped they wouldn't take it into their tattooed, bald heads to come over during the next few days, bringing Mabel with them. It was an unlikely contingency, since they enjoyed comfort and the caravans they usually lay around in would be cold at this time of year. Eric crossed his fingers.

He was ambivalent about the continued presence of the professor and Mrs H., who seemed to be glued to their bar stools, and had got involved in a covertly acrimonious discussion on the rival merits of wooden and fibreglass boats. Neither of them held any particular brief for either form of craft: rather each was concerned to prove that he, or she, was more familiar with the complexities of the matter than the other. It made tedious listening, but they gave the bar something of a lived-in air. He only hoped the professor would not make one of the curious remarks with which he was wont to startle ladies. He supposed the man had some sort of inferiority complex, but it could be embarrassing. Mrs H., too, could swear like a parrot when she felt like it. The girl seemed negligible: the only danger there was that she might start crying.

'What'll you have then?' Eric asked his guests. He was satisfied with all of them except for the one with the golden curls. Mrs H. was already eyeing him speculatively, while he was addressing the brown-haired woman and calling her Jessica as though he'd known her for ever.

'I'll have a brandy,' said Jessica. 'Thanks.'

'And I,' said Jon, thus furthering the impression that he and Jessica were very old and good friends and were in the habit of slugging down pints of Napoleon together. Jessica made no demur since it was possible that she did know him quite well. Off the stage most people looked more or less the same to her so she treated everybody with a warmly respectful

43

informality which was not as easy to practise as it appeared: it had taken some time for her to gauge it correctly, but once perfected was as efficacious as a mask. Nobody really knew Jessica very well.

'Whisky and soda,' said Harry.

'A glass of white wine, please,' said Anita.

'I'll just have water, thank you,' said Ronald.

Another big spender, thought Eric sourly, forgetting for the moment that this water was on the house, and toying with the idea of giving him a glass from the tap.

'So you're all here for Christmas then,' said the professor, twisting round on his bar stool to look at them. 'The island's a fine place in winter,' he added in order to prove that he was familiar with it in all its moods.

'It's better in summer,' said Mrs H., for the same reason.

'I imagine it gets very crowded then,' said Anita. 'I don't think I'd like that. I think everywhere is nicer when the season's over.' She thought of the stationery department in the week before Christmas and felt a small pang of insecurity. It was chaotic but lively and it was hers. She was somebody there. Here she could be anybody. She looked down at her velvet skirt to reassure herself of her identity. 'What do you do?' she said to Ronald as they were standing together, a little apart from the others.

'I'm a psychoanalyst,' said Ronald. This word had the usual effect of creating a pause in the conversations which were going on at the bar, and Ronald wished he'd only said he was a doctor. It was bad enough when he said that, since people sooner or later would slither up to consult him about the side effects of the drug they'd been prescribed, or the pain in the middle of their upper back; but when he said he was a psychoanalyst people, according to temperament, either clamped their jaws firmly shut in case they uttered some remark which would immediately reveal to him that their psyches were in a horrible and unhygienic condition, or expected him to help them sort out their love lives – free.

44

'Goodness,' said Anita.

'And what do you do?' asked Jessica, moving away from Jon, who had drawn her into a confusing exchange involving an experience on location which apparently they had shared and of which she had no recollection.

'I'm a buyer,' said Anita. 'A fashion buyer,' she added, realizing as she spoke that these words had emerged from somewhere in her subconscious where she kept unuttered desires. Ronald would find that interesting, she thought bleakly. Why was it, she wondered, that whenever she was out of her milieu she tended to behave uncharacteristically. Perhaps everyone did. The thought was no consolation, for she had realized at once that even if she grew fond of her fellow guests, and friendly with them, she would not be able to reunite with them in London because they would find out the truth.

'How fascinating,' said Jessica. 'Where?'

'Oh, just one of the stores,' said Anita, for she didn't want this vivacious woman bouncing into the fashion department and demanding to see her in order to get a discount on a little Jean Muir. 'Nowhere you'd know.' What a waste of time. By not adhering to the truth she had now given the impression that she was a person of no real significance, employed in a back-street frock shop. She wished she knew what was wrong with her.

'And you,' said the professor, leaning forward on his bar stool to peer closely at Jessica. 'What do you do?'

Jon stepped forward and put his arm round Jessica's shoulders. 'Come on,' he said, 'you know who *this* is.' But Jessica was not wearing one of her acting faces, nor had she been talking in her commercial voice. There was a rather puzzled silence, not without embarrassment in some of those present.

'Tea for three?' mimicked Jon, quoting the tea-bag commercial in which Jessica was flanked by rival suitors while presiding over a Queen Anne teapot and shadowed by a jardinière holding a ladder fern.

That bloody fern, thought Jessica. It appeared in every commercial, every drama, every sit-com, every documentary, every chat show, every newsreel. It reared its head in living rooms, kitchens, offices, churches, police stations, filling stations, burial parlours, warehouses. It was ubiquitous. No director, no producer would embark on a project without first ensuring that the ladder fern was in place. Jessica had gone so far as to make a fuss, insisting that they must be kidding as they carted in the loathsome foliage; protesting that she couldn't act with that plant, weeping that she was weary of the sight of it; that she and Mike had a game whereby they only watched television together in order to see which of them would first spot the ladder fern and gain a point. What, she had demanded, would happen to their relationship when Mike saw her actually seated beneath it? He'd laugh himself sick. All to no avail. The director had said he was surprised at her: she was well-known and widely appreciated for her lack of artistic temperament, her avoidance of public tantrums. What, he had asked, had come over her? He had been rather cold. And the ladder fern had stayed in place.

She emerged from her bitter musings to hear cries of recognition. One of her ways of coping with this sort of exposure was to remove herself in reverie, but she always had to come out again. It wasn't as bad as it had been at first when off-stage acclaim had made her feel diminished and soiled. Now she had adopted two methods of dealing with it: either she put on an act, or she became exceedingly, exaggeratedly dull – which was also an act but too subtle to be perceived as such.

'So you've come to get away from it all, have you?' said the professor. 'Get away from the bright lights and the roar of the greasepaint. I wondered what a beautiful woman like you was doing down here.'

He's off, thought Eric resignedly, beginning to polish glasses with neurotic speed.

Why, wondered Jessica, couldn't they have had roses, or love-in-a-mist, or chrysanthemums, or even a vase of gladioli, or a cheese plant, or a banana plant, or a potted palm . . .

'Do you want another of those?' asked Harry.

'Yes please,' said Jessica. The atmosphere had altered in some degree now that everyone knew who she was. Only Harry was the same because he never watched television and still didn't know who she was, except that she was the nice woman he had met on the train. Ronald had seen her in *Hedda Gabler* because his wife had hauled him to the theatre: she was always doing that, and had even made him go to *The Phantom of the Opera*. Ronald shuddered at the memory. His wife, when he came to think of it, had actually been far from perfect. Anita knew all about Jessica from reading magazine and newspaper articles. She was thinking it would be sucks to the buyer when she told her who she'd spent her hols with. Eric, as the realization sank in, was beginning to feel a sense of deep gratification. He had not associated the name on the letter which Jessica had sent him with the radiant star of the tea-bags who frequently interrupted his viewing when he found time to watch telly and conditions permitted transmission to the island. That name would add a great deal of lustre to the visitors' book. Jon had always known who she was, and he, of course, knew her better than anybody.

Eric had made the bold decision to seat all his guests at one table without first asking their approval. He had given the matter careful consideration, and having entertained a mental image of five people sitting at separate tables sucking defrosted asparagus stalks in solitary state, he had enlisted Finlay's help in removing the small tables and installing the large, round Victorian one from the parlour where it had taken up too much space anyway. As far as the locals were concerned the restaurant – or, as he preferred to call it, the dining room – would be closed for Christmas. Some of them and several of the incomers would be annoyed by this: they liked to drift in for chicken and chips when they felt like it and couldn't be bothered to cook. They could boil their heads, thought Eric vengefully. The little tables were out in the old stables. Ha. 'Any chance of a meal tonight, Eric?' the professor had asked. 'No,' Eric had said. Ha, Ha. He wondered briefly if all innkeepers detested some of their customers as much as he did.

'Dinner's ready when you are, ladies and gentlemen,' he said. 'There's not a great deal of choice, but what there is is all home-cooked.' He was modestly proud of this speech, which he considered to be frank, open and serenely confident. Finlay's sister-in-law was a more than adequate cook with occasional flashes of inspiration: her soups, broths and *potages* were particularly good, since not only was she Scotch but she had spent a little time working in an *auberge* in Dieppe. Finlay, when he was half seas over at festival times, was apt to remark that she had swum the channel to get there, and then fall down laughing. Eric had never understood why Finlay found this so funny. She also had a way with fish, and her cakes rose in the middle in the proper fashion. She wasn't so good with meat: she made the steak go tough – still, you couldn't go far wrong with a roast, and you couldn't have everything.

For breakfast (seven to nine) the guests could choose between bacon and egg and eggs – boiled, fried, poached, scrambled, *en cocotte*, or flattened into an omelette. Or they could opt for kippers or finnan haddie, or have the continental with hot rolls, which were no trouble to prepare since you just got them out of the freezer and bunged them in the Raeburn for a minute or two, and which always made a good impression; and marmalade or rowan jelly boiled up by Finlay's wife. Such homely little touches made all the difference. Lunch was to be a simple affair of soup followed by ham and cheese and tomatoes and cucumber and things like that

48

because Finlay's sister-in-law went home to rest at midday; but they could have more hot rolls with their soup. If they wanted to go out and wander round the dripping island they could take sandwiches. Everything was under control.

And as for dinner . . .

'Gosh,' said Jessica scrutinizing the typed menu.

'I'll have soup and steak-and-kidney pudding and Queen of Puddings,' said Ronald making up his mind unusually quickly because he was starving and seduced by the word 'pudding'.

'Soup and the mackerel,' said Harry.

'I'll have the steak — rare,' said Jon.

Damn, thought Eric.

'Can I have the grapefruit?' said Jessica, 'only not grilled — just as it is.'

'Me too,' said Anita.

'. . . and the steak,' said Jessica.

'And me,' said Anita.

Eric was tempted to suggest that they would be better advised to stick to the steak-and-kidney which would melt in the mouth (because, to be perfectly truthful, he'd bought it from a butcher's shop on the mainland), but he'd left it too late.

The grapefruit was rather small and bitter. Perhaps they grew them locally, thought Jessica irritably. She was not familiar with the problems of getting fresh and flawless produce on to islands. Turning to talk to Harry she caught sight of a familiar object out of the corner of her eye. Turning fully round in her chair she beheld the ladder fern on a three-legged stool between the windows. She laughed.

'Something funny?' asked Jon through a mouthful of soup.

'Not really,' said Jessica. 'I was just thinking that no matter where you go you can't get away from things.'

Eric, overhearing this, was rather displeased with her. Here she was at the edge of the world with all the seas separating her from all she'd been used to and she didn't seem to be appreciating it properly. He was disappointed in her.

49

'They change the sky, but not their minds, who sail across the sea,' said Harry.

'Who said that?' asked Jon, who could recognize a quote when he heard one.

'Horace,' said Harry.

'Oh yes,' said Jon.

'Are you a teacher?' asked Anita.

'No,' said Harry. 'I'm retired. I was in the army.'

That should have been obvious to anyone, thought Jessica. He had the unmistakable cleanliness of the professional soldier, the military bearing.

'What are you in now?' asked Anita, addressing Jessica because she couldn't think of anything intelligent to say to an old soldier. She had been born after the war.

'I'm not doing anything at the moment . . .' said Jessica, who hated talking about work. She considered it unlucky.

'Resting,' said Jon.

Oh God, thought Jessica, scraping round her grapefruit skin and drifting into a reverie about the scrubbed cleanliness of officers. It was, perhaps, a reaction against the mud and blood of the battlefield, the dismembered limbs, the loosed entrails . . . With her steak before her she wished she'd ordered fish. She sawed at it half-heartedly and beef blood seeped into her broccoli.

Ronald was savouring a slice of suet crust soaked in the sauce, rich with kidney, and thinking that if his wife had been here she'd have made him inquire whether the vegetables were frozen or fresh. He himself cared not a jot one way or the other. He ate half a baked potato and a carrot.

'Did you ever kill anyone?' asked Jon suddenly.

Eric, coming in to remove the plates, was startled by this remarkable query, but the others, aware that it could only be aimed at the soldier in their midst, placidly sat back adjusting their napkins, although they all felt the question was rather uncalled for.

'Oh, hundreds,' said Harry. 'Hundreds and hundreds.' If he had said, no, Jon would have wanted to know why not. It was improbable that, with his apple pie before him, he would go on to probe for details of this mayhem. Jon did open his mouth but Jessica forestalled him, so he put some apple pie in it.

Jessica was not going to sit by and watch her friend being insolently interrogated by the squirt with the curls. 'I'm starting in a play in the West End in the New Year,' she said. She knew this self-sacrificial revelation would hold their interest and only hoped that Harry wouldn't think she was showing off.

'Don't you get nervous?' asked Anita.

'Yes . . .' said Jessica.

'Nobody without nerves can give a performance,' explained Jon.

'There was an actor once,' said Jessica, 'who was always sick when the curtain went up, and one day he said to himself, "Sod this for a game of cards," and he went in for market gardening.'

'Why do you do it?' asked Ronald, wiping a drop of raspberry jam from his whiskers.

'Do what?' asked Jessica, who had been about to go into a dream about cabbages and chrysanthemums and rows of beans.

'Act,' said Ronald. 'Why do you go on the stage if you don't like it?'

'But I do like it,' protested Jessica. 'I feel most myself when I'm being someone else.' She began to wish she hadn't had wine with her dinner, for this was surely a most unwise statement to make to a man who made a living by diving around in the depths of other people's motives and unrealized wishes. He had probably now diagnosed her as an inadequate personality. Ronald too was regretting his question since he didn't really want to know why Jessica went on the stage, and feared, as always, that she would go on to talk at length about herself and her problems, or conversely, avoid him like the plague. Out of his habitat he was beginning to realize that other people's problems bored him stupid. He had allowed himself to become conditioned into asking pertinent questions and it was high time he got over it. It was high time he had a holiday.

'Coffee is served in the lounge,' said Eric.

He went to bed at two o'clock, having rendered the inn shipshape, and half woke in the night, rolling over in bed searching for the warmth of his wife; but she was in Glasgow. Her side of the bed smelled faintly of seaweed.

He was up at six, lighting the fire in the dining room. Finlay's sister-in-law had already let herself in through the yard door and was smoothing rashers of bacon on the chopping board. Eric looked in the freezer to make certain he'd remembered to get kippers and finnan haddie from the fishmonger on the mainland, and went to lay the breakfast table, thus freeing Finlay's sister-in-law to get on with her preparations. He wondered uneasily what he'd do if she contracted a virus or was called away to tend to the dying.

Anita was first in the dining room, having already made herself a cup of instant coffee in her bedroom, utilizing the electric kettle and the little packets provided. Eric regretted the necessity for this discourteous arrangement, but he could not afford to waste time running up and down with trays of early-morning tea. The hot rolls would correct any impression of uncaring on his part. He had also put the butter into pats because he knew everyone hated those tiny foil packages, one of which did not contain enough butter for one slice of toast, while two supplied too much. It was these small touches which made such a difference.

'Would you like your breakfast now?' asked Eric.

'No,' said Anita, 'I'll wait till the others come down.'

'Coffee?' said Eric.

'Well . . . yes, please,' said Anita, standing by the fire and looking down at the newly established glow. She mustn't let herself drink too much coffee since it acted as a diuretic and she wanted to go for a walk.

Harry had already been for a walk along the strand as dawn was breaking and came in with his muffler still round his neck. Ronald and Jessica came down shortly afterwards, but there was no sign of Jon. Eric wasn't surprised: from what he had seen of Jon he would not have expected him to be either thoughtful or punctual. He determined that if Jon came down a minute after nine he could get stuffed. He was prepared to put himself out for those guests who would appreciate it, but if Jon wasn't careful he'd find more in his soup than he'd bargained for. Eric caught himself up: the landlord should not get into the habit of cordially loathing customers or he could drive himself crazy. He must maintain a calm, detached attitude – rather like a psychiatrist – and not permit himself to get upset.

Jon didn't wake until nearly midday, when Finlay's sister-in-law came to make his bed. He crawled from under the sheets stark-naked before half-heartedly draping a towel about his loins. Finlay's sister-in-law was unmoved. If Eric had witnessed this he would have appreciated even more deeply her sterling qualities: a lesser woman might have shrieked and rushed down to insist that the landlord do something about it.

'I think we did the right thing,' said Jessica, standing outside the inn and sniffing the air like a retriever. 'I wondered for a while, but now I'm reassured. The mad lady in the high heels gave me a bit of a turn – I thought there might be more like her all over the island, and she wasn't at all what I was expecting. I wonder who she was?'

'I don't suppose we'll ever know,' said Harry. 'She probably came over in the summer and just stayed on. Hordes of people come over in the summer.'

'Like birds . . .' said Jessica, thinking how alarming it would be if you were a migrant bird and all your fellows suddenly flew off while you were trying to make a telephone call, or find your bra or something. 'You know this island, don't you?' she said to Harry. 'You've been here before.'

'Yes,' said Harry. 'I've been here before.'

'I thought so,' said Jessica, 'when the boatman recognized you.' She had had a brief fantasy in which Finlay had been, not the boatman, but Harry's batman in the war. Some sense which was partly natural to her and which had been partly acquired through the practice of her profession made her aware that she should not pursue the matter.

'I'll show you a bit of the island if you like,' said Harry, grateful for her reserve, and he began to walk along the road he had thought never to walk again in this life. Jessica walked beside him with her collar turned up. There was a cold rain in the air which could at any moment turn to snow.

'We're coming to the Point,' said Harry when they had walked for a while. 'Beyond that head there's nothing until Iceland.' He stood looking out at the sea, and then turned slowly to look inland. A square-built house, half covered in leafless creeper, stood on the first slope of a low hill, gazing with blind windows out at the ocean.

'My wife was born there,' said Harry after what seemed to Jessica, who was beginning to freeze, a very long time. She felt herself grow colder.

'What happened to her?' she asked.

'I took her away,' said Harry. 'I was stationed abroad after the war and I took her with me. She died on the boat home and we buried her at sea.'

'It wasn't your fault,' said Jessica.

'I know . . .' said Harry. He turned towards the sea. 'And some years later,' he added in a conversational tone, 'my son was drowned just beyond those rocks there. He was seventeen.'

Jessica had the sensation of one who has forgotten her lines. 'Oh,' she said.

'. . . and on the face of it,' said Harry, 'that wasn't anybody's fault either. His dinghy capsized, but he could swim like a seal. He must have hit his head . . .'

There was a seal just beyond the rocks. It went under water as Jessica watched. 'Why did you come?' she asked. The question was abrupt, but there are no lines to speak to those in grief.

'I don't know,' said Harry. 'I really don't know.'

'We'd better get back,' said Jessica. 'It's beginning to snow.'

'When we brought him out of the water he looked as though he was asleep. His grandfather buried him . . . did I tell you my wife's father was the minister here?'

'No,' said Jessica, 'you didn't tell me that.'

'Finlay dug the grave. One of his tasks is to dig the graves. Did you know?'

'No,' said Jessica, 'I didn't know.'

'How could you,' said Harry. 'Forgive me. I was thinking aloud.' He had never spoken before of those deaths, but had carried them around with him, secretly strapped to his heart. 'I'm sorry,' he said again. 'I shouldn't have burdened you with that.'

'Don't be silly,' said Jessica absently, wondering why there was no antidote to grief. If a person had a headache, or broke his leg, or developed cancer there was always *something* other people could do – aspirin or whisky or morphia, or just kindness. 'I'm going to buy you a brandy,' she said, since there was nothing else.

She took off her coat in the hallway of the inn and hung it on a peg beside an old fur. She supposed someone had got drunk and forgotten to put it on when she left. There were several people in the bar eating ploughman's lunches. If they eat the ploughman's lunch, thought Jessica idiotically, what will the poor ploughman eat? Eric was offering only soup, sandwiches and the ploughman's in the bar, refusing to burden Finlay's sister-in-law with the necessity to provide chicken in a basket or battered prawns.

'You'll find your lunch laid out in the dining room,' he said as he saw Jessica and Harry. 'Just let me know when you want your soup.'

'There's no hurry,' said Harry. 'Do you know who lives in the Manse?'

'You mean the Old Manse?' asked Eric. 'The minister's been gone for years, I believe, and some chap from London's got it. It's called the Old Manse now. He doesn't usually come down in the winter – comes down in the summer with a load of people for the sailing.'

Jessica wished that Harry hadn't asked this question. The answer, whatever it was, had been bound to be painful. She was imagining a young Harry gathering mussels at low tide with his young love and going home to boil them in the kitchen of the Manse while the minister wrote sermons in his study . . .

'Do you want a brandy?' asked Harry.

Jessica pulled herself together. 'This is on me,' she said, 'and I'm having a Bloody Mary.' She began to imagine Harry and his wife, paddling with their little boy and laughing . . . Impatient with herself she asked, 'Where are the others?' although she wasn't interested.

Eric shrugged. 'Went walking, I suppose,' he said. He didn't care either as long as they weren't late for lunch and he wouldn't be left clearing the table as opening time approached. Despite the relaxed laws he closed the inn in the afternoon. It was quite busy today. The professor, the girl and Mrs H. were back, and several of the locals were downing pints and ham sandwiches. He thought perhaps his luck had changed until he noticed that everyone was looking at Jessica and realized the word had gone round that the island was entertaining a celebrity.

56

'So what did you do today?' asked the professor of Jessica.

'I walked along the shore,' said Jessica.

'You must have passed my place,' said the professor. 'It's down on the left. Next time you must call in.' The girl in the duffel coat glowered. 'This is Amelia,' said the professor as an afterthought.

Jon shot in. 'Where've you been?' he said to Jessica. 'I've been looking everywhere for you.'

'Why?' asked Jessica, startled by his accusing tone.

Jon stared at her suspiciously. Acting innocent, was she? Well, she'd learn he didn't take that sort of thing from his women. '*You* know . . .' he began and then became aware that people were looking at him oddly. 'I've got an idea,' he said, 'for a script – this place gave me the idea . . .'

Oh, *hell*. Jessica had a method for dealing with this sort of thing, but it evaded her. 'You must tell me about it,' she said, and he began to do so. Well, I didn't mean *now*, she thought, not this minute. I didn't mean it at all, and I certainly didn't mean *now*.

'This sounds to me like shop,' said the professor, eyeing Jon's blond curls with dislike. 'We don't allow shop on the island.'

'No, no,' said Eric in an undertone. 'No, no, no. We're not going to have any of that.' He glanced round to check that there were enough large men to sit on people should the need arise and started out from behind the bar.

The locals discouraged violence because it could draw the attention of the police. They only had one policeman on the island, and since they didn't want the number to increase they assisted him *in absentia* whenever they could. It was part of the island mentality. Islanders are used to handling their own problems and resent outside interference. It was only in the season when the bald-headed ones came over that the locals tended to stay discreetly in the background. They were accustomed to disarming those of their number who had had

57

a dram too much and taken it into their minds to shoot their womenfolk – or lifting the hopelessly inebriated out of snow-filled ditches, drying them off and drying them out before hauling them home in tractor-drawn wagons filled with sheep nuts. They treated these eventualities as matter-of-factly as might a mainlander confronted by a person with hiccups and humanely dropping a cold key down the back of his neck, or a caring Muscovite rubbing snow on the nose of a passing fellow citizen who is himself unaware that frostbite is setting in. There was an element of altruism in their behaviour, but it was also very little trouble to assist in these small ways and it kept the authorities at bay. Medical men were not held in high esteem because of their attitude to alcohol.

'I think I'll have a pint,' said Harry. 'What'll everyone else have?' He had stepped between Jon and the professor and was feeling for money in his back pocket: the angle of his elbow forced Jon away to a small but safe distance from the professor.

'My, my,' said Mrs H., and giggled.

Eric leaned over the bar and gave her a look; she subsided. Ronald and Anita arrived in time to be included in the round and the tension faded – largely because neither of them had noticed it.

'It's very beautiful from the top of the hill,' said Anita. 'You can see for miles, except it was a bit misty. I'm quite damp.'

'You need to wrap up,' said Eric. Of course it was a bit misty. It was December. 'There's a place over the brow where they do pony-trekking. You can go right round the top.' He felt he should warn them that the cliff top could be dangerous in the mist: many an unwary beast and occasional holidaymaker had walked thoughtlessly over the edge, but he didn't want to denigrate the island. Anyway, the advantages far outweighed the hazards for those with eyes to see.

'Do you get much crime here?' asked Ronald. His attention

had been caught by the locals in the corner: they looked villainous, and none too clean. The theories of Lombroso was one of his interests. They might be worth re-examining if approached in a judicious, clinical fashion by an impartial person with a deep knowledge of the complexities of the human organism.

'No,' said Eric.

'Murder, incest, rape,' said the professor, laughing. 'Just the usual.'

Ronald, who would have expected nothing less, was not surprised, but Anita looked disconcerted.

'There's very little theft,' said Mrs H. fairly. 'I can leave my cottage open all day and night.' She bore three love-bites on the side of her neck. Tart, thought Eric.

'I'm hungry,' said Jessica to the company at large. 'Are you hungry?' she said to Harry.

Jon watched them go together to the dining room. He did not fear the old man as a rival but he didn't like the way Jessica was ignoring him – playing hard to get.

The professor turned his attention to Anita. 'Do you think women have fantasies of raping men?' he asked. 'Do men have fantasies of being raped by women?'

'I've no idea,' said Anita. The professor reminded her of a man in the accounts department who said this sort of thing at office parties. Her mother would have described it as dirty talk, and while Anita was too modern to use this turn of phrase she found it definitely lacking in romance.

'No,' said Ronald, who didn't need to ponder over the question because he knew the answer. 'Women don't have fantasies about raping men because women haven't got . . .'
He paused as he became aware that this was not his consulting room where such matters were tossed freely about and where he was meticulous in calling a spade a spade, but a public bar.

'Not got a what?' asked Mrs H. brightly.

'They haven't got the barely subliminal libidinous thrust

of the oedipal compulsion which in the vulnerable psyche can lead to the overt and societally unacceptable expression of psychotic malfunctioning,' said Ronald.

'Come again,' said Mrs H., her ardour chilled by this meaningless remark. Ronald was pleased with himself. He had found he didn't like the professor and Mrs H. and he had shut them up with this well-chosen phrase. Already the holiday must be doing him good if he could relax so far as to use his professional expertise to silence people he didn't take to. Obviously he would have to stop short of behaving irresponsibly, but he wondered if perhaps he was acquiring a more developed sense of humour – a quality in which his wife had considered him deficient. He felt himself smiling.

Eric was pleased with him too. He didn't encourage heavy discussions at the bar but anything was better than the way those two had been taking the conversation.

Anita was impressed. She had bumped into Ronald as she walked home from the hill and had found him heavy going. Now she realized that she had underrated him, for here, clearly, was a man both clever and serious. She wondered if he was married.

'What a *crasher*,' said Mrs H. as Ronald walked, head high, to the dining room, Anita at his heels.

'He's a brilliant man in his field,' said Eric. 'World-famous.'

'I've never heard of him,' said Mrs H.

'No?' said Eric. 'Well, we'd hardly expect you to, would we?' which was as about as rude as he ever permitted himself to be to the punters.

'Well, I must love you and leave you,' said the professor, rising from his stool. The girl followed him. Nobody showed any regret.

'The reappraisal of a historical figure always presents a difficult problem, particularly when his history is comparatively recent, and during the intervening years other people have given their own versions of his character and the events of his life – some of them nearer to him in time than others, and those not infrequently hostile to the principles and ideas which guided him through his span on earth. The heroes of yesterday are often mocked and reviled by the rising generation, who are trying by all means to free themselves from the restraints of the past.'

Well, that's true enough thought Harry, but he had never been satisfied with his opening paragraph and kept, as it were, creeping up on it, hoping to take it by surprise and stun it into submission. The next eighty pages, written in his neat, soldierly hand, had steadily improved as he increased in confidence and facility, but the beginning remained intract-able. Then too, how could he convince a largely secular readership of the power and conviction of Gordon's belief in God? They probably wouldn't be interested. Gordon famed, as much as anything, for being an eminent Victorian had been something of an anachronism in his time. What, for instance, would his co-religionists have made of this: 'I find the Mussulman quite as good a Christian as many a Christian, and do not believe he is in any peril. All of us are more or less Pagans. I like the Mussulman; he is not ashamed of his God; his life is a fairly pure one; certainly he gives himself a good margin in the wife line, but, at any rate, he never poaches on others. Can our Christian people say the same?' This approval of Mohammedanism would cause raised eyebrows in some quarters even today, although for rather different reasons. Harry wondered if he was too old to communicate anything at all to the younger generation.

Jessica tapped on his door. 'Oh,' she said, when she saw the papers lying on the table under the window and the fountain pen unsheathed. 'You're working. I'm sorry.' She wondered what he was writing, but was too polite to ask, and stood near the door so that she could not seem to be peering inquisitively at the closely written sheets. 'I'll go away again.'

'No, it's all right,' said Harry. 'I've finished for today.'

'Are you sure?' said Jessica. 'Because I don't want to interrupt but the Greek god is driving me crackers. Jon, I mean. He keeps talking about some time we were on location together and I can't remember it at all. Either I was paralytic or it never happened and it's him who's crackers.' It was possible that she had been engrossed in a performance, concentrating on not forgetting her lines, or agitating herself about Mike or someone, but it was worrying to think that the episode had really happened and she couldn't remember a thing about it. 'I do daydream,' she said.

'Perhaps you see too many people,' said Harry. 'I had a brother in the diplomatic corps who had the same trouble. He said after a while everyone looked exactly the same to him and in the end it didn't matter. He had two expressions – one of serious interest and one of affability, and after he'd listened to the other chap for a minute or two he could tell which one he should be wearing. Then, if he concentrated enough, after a while he'd usually remember who the chap was. He said if you let them do the talking they nearly always talked about themselves.'

'There's a lot of Greek gods around in my business,' said Jessica. 'Dozens of them. I think they should wear labels – like jam. "Blackcurrant: best before 25 Dec. 2000". Did he go far – your brother?'

'To the top,' said Harry.

'You think I'm daft,' said Jessica. 'What are you writing?' She hadn't meant to ask, but Harry made her feel at ease.

'It's about Gordon,' said Harry. 'Chinese Gordon. Gordon of Khartoum,' he added as Jessica looked unenlightened.

'Oh him,' said Jessica. They'd made a film about him with Olivier as the Mahdi. 'Why?' she asked.

'I was just asking myself that question,' said Harry.

Jessica was embarrassed. He was entitled to ask himself questions, but she wasn't. 'I'm sorry,' she said. 'I didn't mean to be nosey.'

'No,' said Harry. 'You can help. What do you make of this?' He turned over the pages and read: 'One day a Moogi Balaam cursed him from the bank of the river and Gordon noted that it was odd that a disaster happened shortly afterwards. He wrote: "I believe that God may listen to the cries for help from the Heathen who know Him not. These prayers were earnest prayers for celestial aid, in which the pray-er knew he would need help from some unknown power to avert a danger. That the native knows not the true God is true, but God knows him, and moved him to prayer and answered his prayer."'

'Well, I call that magnanimous,' said Jessica. 'I'd've been swearing back at the Moogi whatsit myself.'

'I know,' said Harry. 'Gordon was a complex man. He was a Christian but when he was in the hands of the King of Abyssinia, who said, "You are a Christian and an English-man," Gordon said he was just as much an Egyptian and a Mussulman. He believed in reincarnation too . . . am I boring you with this?'

'No,' said Jessica. 'I think it's extremely interesting. I don't know anyone like that.'

'That's the problem,' said Harry, 'I don't think anyone does any more, so how do I paint a convincing picture of a type of man who seems to be extinct? He believed in being cheerful too; he couldn't bear people with what he called the "cruet-stand expression of countenance". Listen: "Why are people like hearses, and look like pictures of misery? It must be from discontent with the government of God, for all things are directed by Him. If by being doleful in appearance it would do any good, I would say, be very doleful; but it does not do any." And on top of that when the King of Abyssinia was rattling sabres at him he told him he was wasting his time because, far from dreading him since his life was in his hands, he would be exceedingly obliged to anyone who would relieve him of that burden . . .'

'Like Humphrey Bogart,' said Jessica. 'In *Casablanca*. Ingrid Bergman's threatening to shoot him and he says, "Go ahead. You'll be doing me a favour."'

Harry did not say that he understood this attitude very well. Reading of men, younger than himself, who had died by one means or another, he was often conscious of feeling only a painful, longing sense of envy.

'Anyway,' he said, snapping the cap decisively on to his fountain pen, 'let's go and see what's for tea.' He noticed, surprised, that he had been needing to talk to somebody about what he was doing, and Jessica felt the sleepy gratification of a child who has been told a story.

Jon had disappeared when they got downstairs and went into the dining room, Harry being careful, as he had learned to be, not to leave an eye on the brooding antlers which dipped above the doorway.

'The awful part about full-board,' said Jessica, 'is that you eat absolutely everything *and* afternoon tea. They'll have to widen the doors to get me out.'

'Yes, isn't it?' said Anita. 'I swore I wouldn't have any tea but it looks too delicious.'

Finlay's sister-in-law, who had returned from her rest, silently added a bowl of her sister's homemade raspberry jelly to the things on the table and went silently back to the kitchen.

'I've never heard her say a word, have you?' asked Anita.

None of them had. Ronald was eating bread and butter, wondering how it was done. Since he had been so well fed and his bed was made for him he had ceased to mind much about his wife. He found this interesting, for the theory was that sexual desire lessened with physical deprivation and increased on four square meals a day. Either the theory was incorrect or he was not normal.

'There's a dance at the village hall tonight,' said Eric from

64

the doorway. 'I know you're mostly here for a rest, but if you wanted a spot of local colour . . .' He looked over his shoulder to make sure that no islander had crept in to listen: unlike some obliging natives the locals resented being called upon to sing and dance for the delectation of the tourist. They were a dour lot, he thought exasperatedly.

Ronald, who was eating a quantity of Black Bun, flinched: a dance at the village hall sounded rather worse than *The Phantom of the Opera*. His spirits lifted as he realized that if his wife had been with him she would probably have made him go: she saw it as her duty to ingest culture whenever and wherever it was offered. There had been an evening of flamenco once in Andalusia . . .

'Will you go?' asked Anita.

Ronald, deep in masochistic reminiscence, did not, at first, appreciate that it was he whom she was addressing. When he did he responded with a vehement *No*. Realizing that this abrupt refusal had caused a startled hush to descend upon the company, he went on to qualify it. 'I don't like dancing,' he explained.

'You wouldn't have to dance, you could just watch,' said Anita.

'I don't like watching dancing,' said Ronald. Anita began to readjust her recently formed assessment of his character and capabilities . . . 'Watching others perform,' said Ronald, who was also aware that he had sounded like a recalcitrant five-year-old, 'is as extrovert an expression of personality as the overt demonstration itself.' He clamped his teeth into a slice of Dundee cake.

'Then you,' said Anita, thinking about this, 'must be an introvert.'

'Yes,' said Ronald, measuredly. 'If we are to accept the validity of the concept and employ its terminology – then yes – I would describe myself as an introvert.' He wasn't too concerned, at the moment, with the obscure niceties of his inner self since he was examining his developing response to the absence of his wife. She wasn't here, and . . . it was really something of a relief. Astonished, he sat with his mouth a little open. A few crumbs of Dundee cake fell into his beard.

'I think *I'll* go,' said Jessica to Anita. 'Shall we go together?' She knew that Harry wouldn't avail himself of the evening's entertainment.

'I'd love it,' said Anita.

Jon, who had decided to adopt the hard-to-get gambit himself, and was sitting by the ladder fern at the furthest point from Jessica, wondered what her motives were. Why was she inviting the shop-lady to accompany her to the village hall? She was even trickier than he had thought. So – if she wanted to play games . . .

Ronald was still gazing into space. He looked profound or half-witted, according to your point of view, as he made a rapid reappraisal of all he had held sacred. He had accepted, without question, that inter-personal relationships were the pivot, the mainstay, the be-all and end-all, the purpose and meaning of all human existence. Now – the *fuck* with inter-personal relationships, he thought, reaching absent-mindedly for the last round of bread and butter. He did not delude himself that he would necessarily continue in this frame of mind, but it was interesting that he had become aware of it.

'I'll see you in the bar at seven,' said Jessica.

'Right,' said Anita.

That evening the bar was as full as ever it was for the time of year. A few locals, Mrs H., the professor and a girl in the duffel coat.

'This is Patricia,' said the professor.

'G and T,' said Jessica to Eric.

'Going to the hop?' asked Mrs H.

'Yes,' said Jessica. 'We thought we might as well. Are you going?' she added out of politeness.

'Me? No,' said Mrs H. She leaned forward and pinched Jessica lightly on the arm. '*He's* going,' she said. 'You want to bet?' She spoke in a whisper.

'Eh?' said Jessica.

'Him,' said Mrs H., 'the professor. He's got his little red scarf on.'

'Oh,' said Jessica.

Mrs H. correctly recognized this as a sign of in-comprehension. 'It's his pulling scarf,' she said. 'When he's pulling birds he wears his little red scarf. In the summer he goes round in his underpants and in the winter it's his little red scarf.'

'But he's with a girl,' said Jessica. She found, to her annoyance, that she too was speaking in a whisper. There was nothing so catching as whispering, except for yawning.

'Ha,' said Mrs H., 'that makes no odds to him. He'll've made a date with three more by the end of the evening. You mark my words.'

'Good heavens,' said Jessica, feebly.

Eric, who had been listening to these whisperings, gave Mrs H. one of his looks. It meant – you're no slouch in that direction yourself, lady.

'I'll have another mineral water, please, Eric,' she said, in her ordinary tone, except that she had pitched it at a more imperious level than usual. Eric wished he was rich, because then he could afford to pour it down her jumper. 'I have to watch my figure,' she said to Jessica, all girls together.

Jessica thanked her stars that the days had passed when someone would have cried at this: 'No, no. Let *me* watch your figure.'

The professor leaned forward on his bar stool. 'You *don't*,' he said. 'Leave it to me to watch your figure.'

Once upon a time, thought Jessica remotely, Mrs H. would have responded, 'Ooh, don't try your wiles on me, you handsome rogue.'

Mrs H. too leaned forward. 'Ooh,' she began, 'don't try . . .'

Jessica, seeing Anita in the hallway, fled before she could hear the end of this. She had once played in a modern version of *Aladdin*, much of the script of which, she felt, could have been written by the people at the bar. Bawdiness she did not object to; just the predictability of the lines.

'There's a moon,' said Anita, 'so we won't need a torch. It's only about half a mile along the road. Eric said he'd take us in the van, but I said we wouldn't mind walking. Do you mind?'

'No,' said Jessica. 'I couldn't half do with a spot of fresh air.'

'It's stuffy in the bar,' agreed Anita. 'Have you got flat shoes on?' The air was cold and salty and clean.

Back in the bar Eric was making conversation with his *bêtes noires*, remembering the words of one of Mrs H.'s friends earlier that year. 'She,' he had said, indicating Mrs H. with a forward motion of his thumb, ''as 'ad every bloke on this island, bar 'im,' whereupon he had indicated with a backward motion of his thumb the pitiful form of Mrs H.'s husband, John. Eric, who did not consider adultery a laughing matter, had frowned upon the friend. Nevertheless the words had been just. Mrs H., thought Eric, who should perhaps have been a minister rather than an innkeeper, was an uncleanly woman, and the professor was an unregenerate chaser of skirt. They both, probably, were incubating dreadful diseases, and if they weren't they doubtless would be before very much more water had passed under the bridge. He would leave their glasses twice the time in the wash.

A group of men in a corner were gossiping and laughing too loudly, like adolescents who have come across something unfamiliar but suggestive and are faintly nervous of it. Eric ignored them contemptuously, serving them in brisk, unsmiling silence when they came to replenish their glasses. They were all locals, but one of them had been away and come back. He it was who had found something – a woman in Glasgow by the sound of it. 'Never knew her name,' he was saying. 'Don't know where she came from . . . ' Eric sniffed scornfully and ran a wet cloth over the bar counter. 'Never saw anything like it,' said the venturer and his cronies sniggered.

Eric wished perversely that Anita and Jessica had not gone to the dance. Not that he wanted their ears to be sullied by the corner conversation, but the presence of ladies – real ladies, unlike Mrs H. – had a freshening effect on a room defiled by loutish behaviour. They resembled a bunch of flowers in their polite purity. Eric realized that his train of thought was taking an unrealistic turn and paused to wonder what the guests really thought of his inn: he hoped that the old soldier wasn't monopolizing Jessica and causing her to be bored. From what he had overheard of their conversation it seemed not improbable, but she appeared content in Harry's company. There was no accounting for tastes and the old boy was undeniably a gentleman. A further rumble of vulgar mirth from the peasants set his teeth on edge. 'You never saw anything like it,' the man said. 'Black rubber and a rose in her . . .' Eric grew horridly alert. There was probably hundreds of women who behaved naughtily in the anonymity of cities, but he couldn't help wondering whether it was Mabel of whom this creature was speaking. He turned away resolutely, determined to think about something else.

'Sex . . .' began the professor, so Eric said he had to change a barrel, and went out to the inn yard for his own complement of fresh air. He stood in the cold watching the moon-path over the sea, and as he watched he saw the form of a boy crossing it from left to right. In the uncertain light he could have been walking on the strand or on the sea, and as Eric blinked he had gone again, into the shadows. A mist was rising.

Harry standing at his window, looking far out, saw nothing but the gibbous moon. Nothing at all.

Jessica was growing sleepy and the noise was growing louder since a young man had arrived with a drum. Earlier the music had been supplied by a record player, and a few couples had jiggled vigorously around in a corner. Jessica and Anita had sat on folding-chairs behind a table drinking canned lager out of paper cups and hoping they had not taken places reserved for local notables; but nobody had confronted them and, indeed, nobody had taken any notice of them. Four girls had provided the cabaret, hopping about over four swords laid on the floor, clad in kilts and bedecked with bits of white heather, and Jessica had supposed that their turn must have required more skill than was immediately apparent, for otherwise why would they have bothered? 'I could do that,' she had said and Anita had not argued. Then another girl had sung the 'Skye Boat Song', unaccompanied, and somebody had recited a work by Burns. It's all very *tartan*, thought Jessica, but not very authentic. Since the locals were clearly not performing for the benefit of tourists she could only imagine that their culture had ossified into self-parody under the influence of the media and a plethora of communication. The most remote and isolated savage, having once seen himself on telly, would find his attitudes to himself and his rites subtly altered, and these people must have been constantly bombarded by reflections and images of Caledonian mores and behaviour. *Sad*, thought Jessica. Hoots mon and Haggis.

The door opened, several more people entered, including Finlay carrying a flute. The drummer put down his sticks, and someone turned the record-player back on. The lights were lowered. The door opened again and someone who looked like Finlay's sister-in-law slid in along the wall.

'Either of you two ladies care to dance?' asked the professor of Jessica and Anita. They declined: Jessica on the grounds that her feet were hurting, and Anita because she was already too hot. 'Let me know when you want to go,' he said, 'and I'll run you back in the Jag.' He shuffled away in time to the music.

'I'm ready for bed,' said Anita. 'I don't want to wait. Shall we walk back?' It was dark outside: the moon hidden in cloud. Jessica tripped against a low wall.

'Oh, that's nice,' she said of the cool air. 'Let's sit here a moment until we get used to the dark.'

The door opened and the professor emerged flanked by two girls. 'Hang on,' he said, 'I've just got to have a pee.' He moved a foot or so from his companions and urinated over the wall on which Anita and Jessica were sitting. Perhaps he hadn't seen them there. Jessica gave him the benefit of the doubt.

A hush followed the racket as the professor's Jag rumbled away along the sea road. All sound had ceased in the village hall behind them. Then there came the strains of a flute: a wild melody, sweet and sorrowful and piercing – and so unfamiliar, thought Jessica, that it could seldom have been heard on the earth before. They waited until it had stopped and the moon had come out from the clouds before they started home, not speaking.

Jessica looked out to sea, and in the light from the suddenly soaring moon she saw dark shapes at the water's edge; so many she thought she must be seeing things. 'Seals,' she said. 'Look. There are hundreds of them out there . . .' but when Anita looked they had gone.

Jon, walking soundlessly behind them on cushioned soles, saw nothing but the white drift of Jessica's cashmere scarf. It covered her brown hair and swathed her pale neck, guiding him through the shadows.

'Do you suppose this place is haunted?' asked Anita the next morning. She had skipped breakfast because her waistband was feeling tight and had joined the others for elevenses. 'I heard noises in the night.'

'People go to the bathroom in the night,' said Ronald.

'I know that,' said Anita rather shortly. 'They weren't those sort of noises.'

Jessica, too, had heard noises in the night: half awake she thought she had heard the handle of her bedroom door being slowly turned, but as she had always locked her bedroom door when alone – ever since her second husband had returned, six months after the divorce, to pick up his pyjamas – she had gone back to sleep. 'What sort of noises?' she asked.

'Sort of people coming and going,' said Anita. 'A lot of people.'

'A lot of people come and go in an inn,' said Ronald.

'Not usually at three and four in the morning,' said Anita, getting cross. 'And I could hear people talking, only I couldn't hear what they were saying.'

'Did you listen?' asked Ronald.

'No,' snapped Anita. He sounded as though he thought she was an eavesdropper. 'I just heard.'

Ronald ate a double triangle of shortbread and watched her thoughtfully. He looked as though he might be going to say something else sensible and Jessica broke in before he could utter whatever it was. There is nothing more infuriating than resolute rationality in the face of the inexplicable, and Jessica was entirely on Anita's side. Whether or not she had heard phantoms in the dark she should not be subjected to the chilly scepticism of the narrow-minded. 'Ghosties and ghoulies and long-legged beasties,' she said, adding lamely, 'and things that go bump in the night.' She sipped her coffee.

Finlay's sister-in-law brought in a fresh pot. She was moving rather more slowly than usual: Anita noticed that she seemed to be limping slightly and bent upon her a look of smiling concern. It was wasted as Finlay's sister-in-law, having put down the coffee pot, was gazing through the window. She lifted a hand and Anita turned to see whom she was waving to. Nobody as far as Anita could tell. The woman was probably the result of too much in-breeding, and wanting in the head.

Jon sat down beside Jessica, in two minds as to whether or not she should be forgiven. He had thought last night when he saw the women climbing into the professor's Jag that they were Jessica and Anita and had dreamed of death. He had been relieved when he realized that they were walking home, although he felt strongly that Jessica should have hung behind and waited for him — but maybe she was shy. But then *he* had waited, lying naked on his bed, for her to come to him. It had been nearly dawn when he had tried her door and found it locked. There was no excuse for that. How would she talk herself out of it if he challenged her? 'What did you do last night?' he asked.

Jessica was thinking about Bannockburn, and the ghosts of Highlanders, and the horrid ways of Sawney Bean and didn't really notice the abruptness of his question. 'What?' she said. 'Oh, I went to the dance . . .' She took another sip of coffee.

'Were you so terribly tired?' he asked. Tiredness would not be a perfect excuse but it was better than nothing.

Jessica looked up at him. She had the feeling that they were at cross-purposes. 'It must have been after midnight when I got to bed,' she said.

So she was still playing with him, laughing at him. He felt his mind clear suddenly as though a great wave had passed over it. If she meant to carry on like that he would show her that in this game he was her master. He laughed, and to a casual watcher it would seem that he relaxed. His beautiful face lost the set smoothness it had worn; small, human lines of mirth appeared at the corners of his eyes, wrinkled the top of his nose. He seemed, in an instant, attractive and full of humour. 'I'll race you to the beach,' he said.

73

Mesmerized, Jessica rose and followed him. Ronald sat with an unchewed mouthful of shortbread. Over the past few minutes he found he had unwittingly made a clear clinical diagnosis: one of his fellow-guests was quite, quite mad – far gone in paranoia and with marked schizoid tendencies. What a nuisance, thought Ronald; but he was on his holidays and there was nothing he could do about it. He swallowed his shortbread.

'Scotland *is* haunted,' said Anita. 'Everywhere there are ghosts of the past.' Finlay came into the room with an armful of logs. 'Is the inn haunted?' she asked him.

Finlay put down his logs and stood, considering. 'Aye,' he said, and went out again.

'There,' said Anita. 'I told you so.'

Jessica ran along the sand after Jon, leaping the ridged sea streams, until it occurred to her that she was getting on a bit for this sort of thing. She wondered what her agent would say if she saw her, and slowed down.

'Tortoise,' said Jon, waiting for her to catch up with him. He took her hand as they walked and let it go before the gesture could seem too intimate. 'There's a deserted house just before the point,' he said. 'Let's explore.'

He led her over the shingle and across the road. The Old Manse stood as she had seen it the day before, blind with an empty, pathetic haughtiness at the top of the slope. 'Come on,' he said as she hesitated.

'I don't . . .' said Jessica.

'Come on.'

Reluctantly she followed him up the path across which trailed bare briars and strands of honeysuckle. She felt uneasy, with a fugitive sense of disloyalty – as though she was trespassing not on the property of the bloke from London who came down with a crowd in the summer for the sailing but on Harry's memories.

'It feels as though no one's been here for years and years,' she said. They stood on the gravel in front of the porch, and then looked through the windows.

'Sitting room,' said Jon. 'Looks as though they haven't made many changes here since the olden days. There's a three-piece suite.' He went to the window. 'Dining room,' he said. 'Come on, let's go round the back.' The small yard behind the house was paved with slate. 'Hallo,' he said. 'Not so deserted after all. Look . . .' There was a row of wet, bare footprints leading to the red-painted back door.

'Oh,' said Jessica. 'Let's go . . .'

'It's only local kids,' said Jon, laughing. 'Tough little brutes – going round with no shoes on in this weather.'

Jessica shivered at the mere thought – at least she told herself that was why she was shivering. 'We'll be late for lunch,' she said.

'It's not midday yet,' said Jon and he laughed again. Jessica wished he wouldn't laugh so much. It sounded out of place in the sorrowful, dignified hush.

'What?' she said.

'It's not even midday,' said Jon. 'Two minutes to midday.' It seemed to Jessica that they had been out together much longer than that.

'Well, I want a drink,' she said, and she thought in her inconsequential way of the noon-day devil who slingeth arrows about.

On the way back she noticed a white cottage down near the shore's edge. 'I suppose that's where the professor lives,' she said.

Jon, who had been humming a tune from *The Phantom of the Opera*, stopped in mid-cadence. 'Prat,' he said venomously. Jessica, unperceptive as ever, heard in this not the sourness of jealousy but only the echo of what appeared locally to be received opinion.

The cottage looked neglected; a few tiles missing from the roof and the garden fence half flattened. Jessica had often

75

wondered whether she was rich enough to invest in a small villa in Tuscany, or a farmhouse in Provence, or even a cottage in the Shires, but now she wondered whether it was not unkind and thoughtless to buy a house only to leave it alone much of the time and fail to look after it properly. She wondered whether it even made economic sense and whether it was not wiser to take your ease in small hotels, which if not perfect, did not require you to re-tile the roof or maintain the grounds.

They were still talking about ghosts in the bar. '. . . and one room which was always freezing cold even in the middle of summer,' Anita was saying.

'Probably rising damp,' said Eric.

'Don't you believe in ghosts?' asked Anita.

'I've never seen one,' said Eric.

'No, but do you believe in them?' insisted Anita.

'Since I've never seen one, I don't see why I should,' said Eric.

'You've never seen an electric current but you believe in them, don't you?' said Anita.

'That's different,' said Eric.

'There is undoubtedly a phenomenon known as projection which under certain circumstances might appear to take on corporeal substance,' said Ronald.

Anita wasn't sure what he meant by this, but it sounded as though he was on her side, and she warmed to him again.

'It need not even necessarily be seen as a function of hallucination,' added Ronald.

'Oh, by the way,' said Eric as he caught sight of Jessica, 'there was a phone call for you earlier. They said they'd ring back.'

'But nobody knows where I am,' said Jessica.

'Somebody does,' said Eric.

Jon listened carefully.

'What did they say?' asked Jessica.

'Just that they'd ring back,' said Eric. When he'd heard a female voice he had thought for a moment that it might be Mabel.

'Does anybody realize that tomorrow is Christmas Eve?' asked Anita. 'I'd almost forgotten – it's so peaceful here.'

'They don't bother much with Christmas – the islanders,' explained Eric. 'They celebrate New Year, Hogmanay.'

The said celebrations encompassed a week, during which barely a living soul took a sober breath.

'That's why this is a good place to get away from it all,' said Eric. 'It doesn't happen.'

'I think it's going to snow, though,' said Anita. Perversely, she was missing the atmosphere evoked by robins and shepherds and fat-tailed sheep: there wasn't so much as a sprig of holly to be seen.

'If it does,' said Eric, 'there's a couple of pairs of skis in the old stable, and some good slopes on the other side of the island.' The skis had been left by the previous owner, who wouldn't need them on the Costa del Sol, where he had gone to end his days sunnily and cheaply.

'I was still hoping to get in a bit of sailing,' said Jon.

'You must be crazy,' said Jessica involuntarily, chilled by early memories of grey, heaving seas; trying to sleep in salt, wet blankets in a space half the size of a coffin, boiling cans of soup on a tilting stove, and trying not to go to the lavatory because what they referred to as the 'heads' was two inches away from the table where the rest of the party would be endeavouring to eat its soup before it pitched itself on to the floor – or, as her father would have insisted, 'the deck'. Jessica was not being personal, nor unusually perceptive, when she accused Jon of insanity: she thought the same of anyone who chose to spend time at sea when nothing actually compelled him to.

'Most you can do this time of year is doddle round the

coast in a dinghy,' said Eric, 'and even that's a bit dodgy. Fishing vessel went down with all hands this time last year.'

'That was a submarine,' said Mrs H., coming in from the cold and removing her fur gloves. 'Fouled her nets and took her under.'

'That's what some say,' interrupted Eric, not because he doubted the theory, but because he liked interrupting Mrs H. 'According to the locals ships have been going down there since the year dot.'

'Giant squid, I suppose,' said Mrs H.

'I've sailed a four-masted Baltic schooner through a typhoon in the China Seas,' said Jon improbably. Nobody bothered to challenge this statement and even Jon saw that he would do well to qualify it in the interests of plausibility. 'Well, it was more of a squall, actually,' he said, 'and there were five of us.' Nor had this squall occurred in the China Seas: it had happened off the Hook of Holland with a hired crew to man the vessel, and a camera crew to immortalize the image of Jon shinning up the rigging to the crow's nest where there awaited a maiden clad in Dutch bonnet and clogs, holding tantalizingly aloft a platter of fishfingers. In the end this scene had actually been shot ashore with special effects, but Jon *had* hung in the rigging for a while until the director had given it up as a bad job. The commercial had been shown only on the continent, where they had lower standards. 'We were research-ing for a film,' explained Jon. 'Only it was going to go so far above budget that they gave it up.'

This could have been true and Jessica was disposed to be sympathetic, for she knew too well the broken promises, the blighted schemes, the failed hopes attendant on film-making. 'Poor you,' she said.

The others, who were not conversant with the inflated enterprises, the hazards and the sheer financial lunacy of this business, remained sceptical, and Jessica found herself moment-arily at a small remove from the company, isolated with Jon

78

in a shared appreciation of the fantastical, the unreal elements of their common profession.

'Do you suppose there *are* any giant squid?' asked Anita, trying to bring the conversation down to a more practical level and out of the Munchausen realms of fevered exaggeration and falsehood.

'There are recorded instances,' said Ronald, 'but I can't remember the exact dimensions of the largest. Down in the lowest depths are things we may never learn about. It's quite possible that mankind will know more of the furthest galaxies than it will ever know about the creatures of the sea. It may be easier to fly beyond the stars than plumb the depths.' He became aware of the metaphorical psychological implications in this observation and lapsed into reverie clouded by self-doubt. If he followed the metaphor through and it held, then it was to the visionaries, the mystics – even the religious – that the human race must turn in its search for enlightenment, while he and his kind continued poking round with a stick in the mud at whatever level they could reach. This disheartening reflection kept his attention until teatime.

The professor entered alone, which made him look a little strange, like a person who habitually wears glasses but has mislaid them, or a woman without her make-up.

'On your own?' asked Mrs H. 'Not got a girl today?'

'Several,' said the professor complacently. Jessica supposed that he'd left them to cook lunch in the cottage by the sea. One would be saying, '. . . he doesn't care for too much pepper', and another would be saying, '. . . he likes his carrots raw', and a third would be saying, '. . . that's too much chutney', and a fourth would be washing her stockings in the sink while a fifth tried to drain the spaghetti . . .

Intent on the choreography of the scene she didn't hear the professor offering to buy her a drink until he repeated himself. He leaned over her and she noticed that he smelled of cooked meat.

'Oh, no, thanks,' she said and he moved down to the other end of the bar to try it on with Anita.

'Does he try it on with absolutely everyone?' Jessica asked Eric.

'Yes,' said Eric.

'He must get a lot of refusals,' said Jessica as she saw Anita also making a negative gesture.

'It's like this,' said Eric. 'I've known other blokes the same. I said to one of them once what you just said to me – you must get a lot of refusals – and he said yes, he got a lot of refusals but he got a lot of acceptances too. If ninety per cent of all the birds in the world turned him down, that left ten per cent, and it's still a hell of a lot of birds. It's like selling double-glazing. You knock on a thousand doors and in nine cases out of ten it's slammed in your face. Then you score. There's a lot of money in double-glazing.'

'Doesn't give you AIDS, though,' said Jessica.

'What doesn't give you AIDS?' asked Jon, returning from the gents.

'Double-glazing,' said Jessica.

'I'd love to see a giant squid,' said Anita.

'You should come scuba-diving with me,' said the professor, who was irrepressible.

'I do scuba-diving,' said Jon competitively.

Poor little soul, thought Jessica. He was so desperate for the limelight he'd admit to anything. She thought she might take his education in hand: teach him how to show off without alienating people; explain to him that nice men didn't go scuba-diving, that scuba-diving was the modern aquatic equivalent of Old-Tyme Dancing, a pursuit followed by people who knew no better, and who frequently owned caravans or fibreglass boats. She was beginning to feel protective towards him.

The phone rang in the hall. 'It's for you,' said Eric to Jessica. 'You can take it at the reception desk.'

'Hallo,' said Jessica and was answered by a crackle as of some toothless being grinding cornflakes between its jaws. 'I can't hear you,' she said. 'Ring back.'

The phone rang again and the crackle again assailed her ears. 'It's no *good*,' said Jessica. 'Who is this?'

'It's me,' said an unrecognizable voice through the cornflakes. 'Listen.'

'I *am* listening,' said Jessica. 'All I can hear is crackling.'

'. . . trouble . . .' said the voice. '. . . careful . . .'

'What?' said Jessica. 'Who are you? What trouble? Oh, *damn!*'

The phone crackled frenziedly.

'You'll have to try again later,' said Jessica, projecting her voice as to the furthest corners of the auditorium and nearly deafening her agent who could hear *her* perfectly clearly.

'Oh sod it,' said her agent to the liar who was standing by. 'I tried. I won't have time to ring again before I get the plane. I only hope she's got the sense she was born with.' For the agent, in her omniscient fashion, now knew where Jessica had gone and that Jon had followed her to her secret destination. It had come through on the grapevine, a more efficient medium than BT.

'She's not stupid,' said the liar.

'No, but you never know with islands,' said Jessica's agent obscurely.

'Can I get you anything?' asked Eric.

Jon was poised with his head inclined to where Jessica was speaking on the telephone. He looked as though he was listening with more than his ears and Eric was uncomfortably reminded of himself. Just so had he sometimes listened from behind the bar when Mabel was talking to the men: unable to hear, yet listening with his whole body.

'No,' said Jon as Jessica came back into the bar.

Murder, thought Eric. When he had been forced to listen like that, wary and tranced, the prospect of murder had often

81

come into his mind. He only hoped that, at the time, he had not looked as crazy as Jon was looking now. The spectacle of another man in the throes of jealous suspicion was almost enough to cure you. Eric was glad he hadn't killed his wife since such an action would have revealed to the world, not only that he couldn't cope with her moods, but that he feared himself cuckolded. It would, without a doubt, have stripped him of dignity. Only Latins, mad people and the local drunks, thought Eric severely, went round killing their women. He remembered, uneasily, times when he had lurked in bushes to observe what Mabel was up to, and vowed that if she returned he would change his attitude. He would make his position clear in a calm and authoritative way and say no more.

'Well,' said the professor, rising to perform his habitual leave-taking as no one was talking to him. 'I must love you and leave you.'

Everyone wondered crossly why he stuck to this outmoded form of words.

'In January 1876, Charles George Gordon wrote: "I would that all had the assurance of future life ... No one is indispensable, either in this world's affairs or in spiritual work. You are a machine, though allowed to feel as if you had the power of action. When things turn out in a way we do not wish, we quarrel with God when we feel put out. Most difficult is this lesson, and only to be learned by a continual thought of this world being only a temporary one – i.e. by continually thinking of death as a release."'

Harry contemplated these words, trying to put out of his mind the part he understood and concentrate on the part he didn't. He had long thought of death as a release, but he wondered what precisely Gordon had meant by the term 'machine'. He had grown increasingly interested in Gordon's cast of mind and less in his campaigns – a symptom of age, considered Harry impartially, wishing that he had himself died in battle when he was young enough to face the final change with vigour and a positive acceptance, rather than the weary resignation which was all that was left to him.

When Jessica knocked at his door he felt the relief of the author interrupted in the midst of a welter of fruitless speculation, when inspiration has ceased and the mere application of the brain seems insufficient to get the pen moving again.

'Am I a person from Porlock?' asked Jessica who was no different from anybody else in that she rather enjoyed disturbing people who were attempting to work. There was not any malice in the urge: it was a primitive, tribal response to the individual intent on private concerns – 'Kindly rejoin the community and let us play.' The man engrossed in solitary pursuits is always a little threatening.

'No,' said Harry, 'or if you are you're welcome. I've had enough for today.'

'How's it going?' asked Jessica, reassured. She sat down in a wicker armchair covered in Eric's cut-price chintz, and ate an apple she'd saved from lunch. 'The awful thing is,' she said, 'that the more meals I get put in front of me the more I eat in between them, and what's worse I can't seem to stop talking about it. Have you noticed that when one stays in an hotel one's powers of conversation desert one and one grows boring? Do you think it's because one eats so much?'

Harry, who had not taken lunch, had been reading with sympathy of nineteenth-century army rations in Egypt – tinned soup, tinned beef or mutton and biscuits – and later of the inhabitants of the garrison of El Obeid who had dug up the buried carcases of dogs, donkeys and camels; had stripped the leather thongs from the native bedsteads, soaked and eaten them; had dug up the rotting gum which the fleeing merchants had buried for safe-keeping, and eaten that; had killed and eaten the vultures, carrion crows and kites, and –

it was hinted – had fallen upon the burial grounds of their own kind, long dead, and had disinterred and eaten them too.

'Did you have lunch early?' asked Jessica. 'You'd gone by the time we got there.'

'I wasn't hungry,' said Harry.

'Nor was I,' said Jessica, 'but I ate it all the same. Perhaps I starved to death in a previous incarnation and I'm trying to make up for it now.'

'Perhaps,' said Harry.

Jessica was disconcerted: she wasn't used to having her thoughtless fantasies taken seriously by people she respected.

Harry sighed, alarming Jessica who imagined that she really wasn't wanted and had intruded on some profound and nourishing solitude: but Harry was thinking of Gordon and his elusive views, as seemingly incompatible with Victorian Protestantism. 'I think,' Gordon had written, 'that this life is only one of a series of lives which our incarnated past has lived. I have little doubt of our having pre-existed; and that also in the time of our pre-existence we were actively employed.' Gordon had greatly valued active employment. 'If we are reincarnated,' said Harry, 'it's unfortunate that we can't remember the details of past lives. It would make writing history a lot simpler.'

'Is that what you're writing?' asked Jessica. 'A history book? I thought it was a biography, but then if the subject's been dead for ages I suppose it's more or less the same thing.'

'More or less,' agreed Harry, wondering how the Victorians had so easily entertained the concept of the soldier as Christian gentleman, and whether Gordon had lived up to the ideal: on the evidence it seemed that he had. Harry, in his youth, had aspired to the same condition, but war had disillusioned him. He didn't know whether this was due to his own inadequacy or whether it had been the climate of opinion that enabled men to become heroes with a clear conscience and to continue in the ways of belief. With all the years of final peace the soldier had lost his accepted purpose, the national acclaim and respect that had been his due; had reverted to the state of the mercenary or become a stealthy feral creature, camouflaged, and alien to the mass of society: his weapons no longer mere extensions of his limbs but complex aspects of a murderous technology. With warfare and mass destruction dependent on merely political decisions, the psychopathy of rulers and the pressure on a button, the simple soldier-man was useful only in conflicts too foreign or insignificant to merit such drastic measures. Inevitably this meant that he would be involved in the unjust suppression of the innocent in foreign lands. Revolution against tyranny was a matter for indigenous populations – or anyway, that was how Harry saw it. It devalued, in retrospect, all that he had lived for. Harry tended to identify, when he thought about it, more with the brutal and licentious soldiery than with his peers who had gone on to positions in industry, banking and Parliament, nor could he identify with the polished pageantry of the Brigades. There was no longer a mess in the world where he would have felt at home.

'But then – if we'd been earthworms,' said Jessica, 'we wouldn't have much of interest to remember, would we?'

'No,' said Harry.

'Most people say they want to come back as a pussy-cat,' said Jessica, 'specifying, of course, that they should be well cared for and beloved and not thrown to the bad dogs.' She was feeling depressed and inclined to jabber meaninglessly. She had awakened early to a dull, grey sky, hanging over the dull grey island, while the dull, grey sea whinged fitfully at its shore. All this presented a melancholy enough appearance, but still was not sufficient to account for the lowness of her spirits. She supposed she must be missing Mike more than she had realized, for if it wasn't that, there must be a different cause: she had suffered no other recent loss and the time had not yet come to fear death, not as far as Jessica was concerned.

She had told herself she was too old to wish for snow and reached out for *The Tenant of Wildfell Hall* in order not to think about the next topic in her train of thought. If she had lain there brooding, she would have understood that she was missing the preparations for Christmas, and since she had gone to such lengths to avoid them it would have made her feel a fool.

'I'm going for a walk,' she said, remembering that the sea was less boring when you got close to it than when it lay around like a wet rug. There would be details of spume and wave and twisted driftwood, shells and the bodies of wind-torn sea birds.

'I might follow you later,' said Harry. 'I'll tidy up these papers first.'

'I'm going along the shore as far as the church,' said Jessica, 'and then up the hill.'

When she went downstairs she saw Jon leaning in the bar doorway. 'Heigh ho,' she said. He took this as an invitation to join her and stepped forward, reaching for his jacket which hung on the hall rack. Jessica didn't really mind, having no particular desire, at the moment, to be alone: she hoped he was prepared to think of something to talk about since she could not – except for Helen Huntingdon whom she was finding increasingly annoying but who, she felt, would not serve to sustain a conversation with Jon. Jon, thought Jessica, did not look the intellectual type. She wondered if he'd ever gone to school.

There was a sifting of snow on the hill tops. 'I wish the snow would come down here,' said Jessica.

'You're a child,' said Jon. He spoke indulgently but she couldn't take offence at what he said, even though he was at least fifteen years younger than she was.

'I sort of expected snow,' she said, sounding, to her own irritation, childish. She was beginning to notice that Jon had an odd ability to guide her responses: it was he who had caused her to gallop along the sands like a two-year-old. 'On the other hand,' she said, 'snow can be most inconvenient.'

'In the Arctic . . .' began Jon, and she feared he was about to spin a yarn, but he was careful. 'In the Arctic,' he went on, 'they think of Hell as cold.'

'I do myself sometimes,' said Jessica, 'when it *is* cold. When I'm too hot I think of Hell as hot. I suppose it's only natural.' She hadn't meant to sound dismissive, but Jon flexed his fingers, unseen in his pockets.

'Do you think the sea will ruin my boots?' asked Jessica after a short silence, gazing down at the Spanish leather.

'Not unless you walk in it,' said Jon and fell silent again.

Jessica began to look beautiful. She could not have explained how she performed this feat, but it was something she often did when people were displeased with her. At the same time she observed aloud that there were a couple of Highland kine in a distant field. Jon, of course, took this as a sexual advance and relaxed, putting an arm around her shoulders: he laughed and drew her closer to him.

Hell's bells and buckets of blood, thought Jessica resignedly, inwardly deploring the multitudinous complexities and resultant misunderstanding inherent in human intercourse. All she had wanted was to go for a walk and exercise away some of the consequences of three meals a day, with added snacks, and already she had nearly quarrelled with a comparative stranger who now showed every sign of being about to make love to her. It could only be due to some deep flaw in her character – or possibly sheer thoughtlessness.

The church had been deconsecrated some time ago, since it lacked both minister and congregation, and was now used as a boat-shed, being conveniently adjacent to the sea. It reminded Jessica of an unfashionable and discarded hat, than which there is nothing more redundant. The road wound round it and up the hill towards the thin toupee of snow which now reminded Jessica of an actor with whom she had once worked in *Nicholas Nickleby*. She determined not to mention this since she knew it would sound winning and give a further wrong impression. They passed an untidy and ill-assorted gathering of gorse, rhododendron, bramble, clematis and infant pine imprisoned in a deep hollow at the roadside. The ham-fisted hand of man was evident here as the wild, the cultivated and the transplanted strove for dominance in a gladiatorially herbaceous fashion. They also made Jessica think of a number of legitimate, illegitimate and stepchildren competing for attention as they struggled up towards the light. Man sows discord, thought Jessica, but she said: 'Crikey, here's some ragged robin in flower. What can have possessed it to come out at this time? It's positively months premature.'

'That's one of the things I like about you,' said Jon. 'When people ask me what I see in you I say, "She knows about wild flowers, she knows their names and where to find them, and when they come out."'

Jessica, who had been having enough trouble finding things to say, was struck dumb at this. Her first thought was that, in fact, she knew virtually nothing about wild flowers and that, anyway, her ragged robin was probably scarlet campion or even maiden's bedstraw, or a spray of earl's evil: she had learned to distinguish dandelion from coltsfoot during the course of a documentary on a tract of countryside for which she was doing the voice-over, and she had an average ability to recognize wild roses and may-blossom and such-like seasonal blooms, but she was far from familiar with the more esoteric flora which lurked shyly in ditches or blew in far-flung meadows and was truly entitled to the term 'wild'. As to the little pink number shivering at the roadside – any fool could have told that it was no time for it to be out. Her next thought came in the form of a question – who the hell would be asking Jon what he saw in her, and why? A faint wisp of memory floated into her mind and away again before she could grasp it, elusive as a dandelion clock. Then she thought, without anger, since the whole thing was too curious to be infuriating, that it was the most terrible cheek on the part of everyone concerned to discuss her at all in relation to Jon whom she'd never met before; and positively cosmic cheek on the part of Jon to ascribe her attractions to a facility for naming plants when she was really quite famous, very amusing and often looked beautiful. She decided he must be mad.

The road levelled above the hollow before beginning its ascent to the hill's summit.

'I think we've gone far enough,' said Jessica, turning to look down at the sea and noticing a gorse bush which had also gone mad and burst into flower in December: she didn't draw Jon's attention to this phenomenon since that might have led him further into a baffling discourse on her horticultural skills. The only explanation she could think of that would make sense of the situation was that, once, she must have got very drunk in a rural setting and Jon had been among those present as she leaped about naming flowers. It seemed implausible, but she'd done a few unlikely things in her time.

'Oh no,' said Jon. 'No. Now we've got this far we must go to the top. Come on, I'll hold your hand.'

'You must be joking,' said Jessica. 'It's at least ten miles to the top and uphill all the way.'

'No,' said Jon, 'no more than two.'

'I don't care,' said Jessica. 'I'm not going up any more hills. I'm going down. I want my tea.' Involuntarily she looked up and saw his face.

'All right,' said Jon, after a moment. 'Race you to the bend.' He won easily as Jessica didn't run but walked behind wondering who had spoiled him to the point that to be thwarted in so small a matter should make him look like murder.

The bar was unusually busy that night. It would be, thought Eric, when he had so much to do in preparation for the next day: he resented the presence of the islanders, who contributed little to his income, when he wanted to look after the comfort of his guests, who would, if he got it right, return to civilization singing his praises to their wealthy friends. 'Did you have a nice day?' he asked Anita, who was sipping a half of shandy.

'It was very interesting,' she said.

Eric was gratified to hear this, for over the past few days he had been contending with a suspicion that Mabel was right; the island was possibly the most dreary collection of rock on the face of the globe and he had made an error in coming here.

'I'm thinking of buying some of the local produce,' said Anita.

'Pardon?' said Eric: what local produce there was – hedgerow jam, jars of mustard, tea-cloths, mugs – was made in English and foreign factories, appropriately labelled and imported to the island; as it was, indeed, to those villages where tourism flourished all over the Isles of Britain and the Western world. Surely a person who had made commerce her profession could not have been so deluded as actually to purchase any of this rubbish.

'The knitwear,' said Anita, 'the local knitwear.'

'Oh,' said Eric. As far as he knew the local knitwear was also imported.

'I walked for miles,' said Anita, 'and I saw a woman sitting by a cottage window, knitting, so I stopped to ask directions to the castle ruins and she asked me in and gave me a cup of tea. She'd just started knitting on these huge needles so I asked her what she was making and she said it was a sweater for her man. She said each village on the island and round the coast on the mainland used a different pattern so that when the men were drowned and washed up on the shore they could tell where they'd come from and take them home to be buried.'

'Oh,' said Eric again. It sounded improbable: the story of the different patterns might once have been true enough, but he doubted that any of the local women still knitted with that practical if macabre purpose in mind: most of them went to the mainland and bought their men's sweaters in Marks and Spencer. Either Anita had encountered an incomer who had fled like himself from the world and was planning to build up a cottage industry (and good luck to her, he thought) or she had met a genuine local who was making a blanket or a matinée jacket for the next jumble sale and was telling lies.

'I thought I might take a few back and try them out as a special line,' explained Anita, who, now that she was away from the pressures of work, was beginning to feel more confident of both her talents and her stamina: so far from her department anything seemed possible and if she returned with a brilliant idea and the goods to back it up she might truly get herself transferred to one of the fashion sections and became truly powerful.

'You could try, I suppose,' said Eric, wondering whether it would be more charitable to leave her with her delusions or advise her now to remember to snip out the labels bearing the legend 'Made in Taiwan'. He decided to say nothing.

Mrs H. appeared in the bar wearing tight jeans and a nylon blouse under her anorak. She was followed by the professor and a girl in the duffel coat. 'We've come from the Crown and Thistle,' she said. 'It was so crowded in there we could hardly breathe.'

The Crown and Thistle was the next pub along the coast, and while it too was run by an incomer it attracted many more of the locals than Eric's, far superior, inn. It had fruit machines and a pool table. Eric felt the bewildered wrath of the simple, virtuous maiden, modestly conscious of her worth, who is rejected in favour of the painted, flouncing fire-ship, all empty promise and implicit hazard. Certainly he did not, at the moment, wish to see his own bar filled to capacity with sweating revellers, but nor did he want to hear about the one up the road.

'Nice, was it?' he asked.

'No,' said Mrs H. 'Much too crowded. You can't *breathe* in there. I'm going to have a half of bitter as it's Christmas.'

Eric looked at her carefully. Since she usually drank water he had always assumed that she was an ex-alcoholic. So far he had not had that kind of trouble with her: she was an undeniably ghastly woman, but – Eric touched the wood of the counter – she had not yet gone on a bender in his bar. He took his time and served her begrudgingly.

The professor also broke his habitual rule and ordered a real lager, although still with lime.

'Pushing the boat out?' inquired Eric with concealed sarcasm. 'Christmas comes but once a year,' he answered himself. There were no signs in the bar that it had come again: no tinsel, paper chains, or holly . . .

'You've got no mistletoe,' said Mrs H. 'Christmas isn't Christmas without mistletoe.'

'We're not doing Christmas,' said Eric. 'That's the whole idea.'

'I think that's letting the side down,' said Mrs H. Her remark might have puzzled a person who was familiar neither with Mrs H. nor with the ways of the island: he might have supposed her to mean by 'the side' all of Christendom and its long traditions: he might have imagined Mrs H. herself to be a woman of religious susceptibility, but he would have been mistaken. By 'the side' Mrs H. meant the English contingent, the visitors and incomers: she had as strong a tribal sense as the islanders themselves, which was one reason for the mutual and cordial, if lightly hidden, detestation which characterized what dealings they had with each other. If questioned, Mrs H. would have said that it was all a matter of 'class', since her vulgarity had corrupted even her deeper human awareness. She considered the islanders' failure to observe the seasonal rites to be evidence, not of a residual paganism, but of a swinish ignorance of the 'done thing'.

'I've put up my little tree and the fairy lights,' she said, 'and I've left John stuffing the turkey. He's a marvellous cook.'

Eric said nothing: he wanted to talk of pudding and flaming brandy, and he did not care to picture the poor cuckold bent over a dead turkey, his hands greasy with corpse fat, while his wife sought diversion in crowded places. Oh, Mabel . . .

'I wanted a rest from all that this year,' said Anita. 'I usually make such an effort – I buy everything fresh and I spend hours peeling and chopping and making gravy – I just wanted a change this year.' She always entertained a few elderly girls from the store and, when they were available, a few men who hadn't been invited anywhere else.

'Hallo,' said Ronald. He was standing close behind her so that as she turned his beard brushed her upturned face. 'Where did you get to today?' He liked to hear a woman talking about cooking and he liked Anita's modest dress of dark paisley wool under a cream-coloured cardigan. He liked her low-heeled shoes and her lightly lacquered dark-red hair. It could well be true, he thought, that red hair was evidence of spirit in a woman, for he had noticed that, at one point, she had grown quite impatient with him. He could not be expected to know that Anita's hair was dyed and that once a month she sat for an hour with her head in a plastic bag to set the colour.

'I went as far as the village,' said Anita. 'I met a local woman knitting a sweater for her man . . .'

Eric was summoned by the professor ordering a second lager, alcohol-free this time.

'Where's Jessica?' asked the professor with the confident grin of the ageing flirt, still unaware that his very confidence makes him look silly.

Jon, sitting a little away from the rest, heard him and stiffened.

'She's standing right behind you,' said Eric. Jessica had

entered a moment before and was waiting for a chance to approach the bar counter.

'Good evening, everyone,' she said in her commercial voice.

'There you are,' said the professor who did not, however, offer to buy her a drink.

'Two brandies, Eric,' said Jon, slipping from his stool and contriving, as it were, to surround Jessica in the way the male positions himself beside the female who is his possession.

'What did you do today?' asked the professor of Jessica.

'We walked to the top of the island,' said Jon before she could open her mouth.

'Enjoy it?' asked the professor, still addressing Jessica, and somehow managing to give a lewd connotation to this simple query.

'She loved it,' said Jon. 'She told me the names of all the trees and flowers and birds.' He smiled down at the top of Jessica's head and slid his hand further over her shoulder towards her breastbone.

Birds? thought Jessica. She could recognize a bird when she saw one, largely because they had the habit of flying around in the air: she could tell a pigeon from an owl; and then there were robins and seagulls, and ostriches of course, and parrots and ducks – although, now she came to think of it, ducks weren't really like birds at all; they were like – well, *ducks*. And trees. Trees looked like very large weeds and from a distance some of them looked like broccoli. The broccoli that Eric served at dinner had resembled a felled tree as it lay on her plate in the blood, but she couldn't positively identify many trees: laburnums when they were flowering, oaks when they bore acorns, willows when they wept – but not many more . . .

'Have you noticed my fir?' asked the professor. Jessica, emerging from the sparse and anonymous forests of her imaginings, misunderstood him. Fur? Was he speaking of his own body hair? Was he perhaps a werewolf? Or was he drawing attention to some unappreciated mink, ocelot or garment of beaver?

'. . . planted it years ago,' he was saying. 'Whipped off the tinsel and the gewgaws, stuck it in the garden and now it's nearly sixty feet tall.'

Ah, thought Jessica, reassured – a *fir*. She could identify Christmas trees. She looked round for an empty table at which she could sit and saw Harry by the sea-facing window: he was looking through it into the darkness.

'May I join you?' she asked in her natural voice. 'How is General Gordon?' She sat down opposite Harry and drew in her chair. 'You didn't come for a walk. I expect he was too engrossing. You must tell me; but first I must tell you what Helen Huntingdon's done now. Shall I?'

'Do,' said Harry.

Jessica leaned closer. 'She put tartar emetic in Arthur's wine,' she said in a low, confidential tone.

'She *didn't*,' said Harry.

'She *did*,' said Jessica. 'Not enough to kill him – just enough to produce nausea and depression.'

Harry glanced round, then leaning towards Jessica he asked in a whisper: 'Who is Arthur?'

'Her little boy,' explained Jessica, also in a confidential whisper.

To the watchers at the bar it seemed that the two of them were deep in an intimate discussion of common friends: which was what Jessica had intended. Harry had entered into the spirit: it was many years since he had played games with a child, but he had not forgotten how. Jessica knew what he was thinking and didn't care: it was one thing to be considered a child by Jon, who by the term had meant 'babyish', and quite another to be seen so by Harry who had sufficient insight to realize that all acting was game-playing and that therefore all actors were, by definition, children. At least when they were on stage, amended Jessica in her mind.

'Her husband was just like my second one,' she explained. 'Pissed as a rat *all* the time, and he was trying to make a man of Arthur by teaching him to drink and swear.'

'How old was Arthur?' asked Harry.

'About six, I think,' said Jessica.

'Good Lord,' said Harry.

'So, she kept giving him wine, and gin, and brandy and water with tartar emetic in it, and she'd say, "Arthur, if you're not a good boy I shall give you a glass of wine," or, "Now Arthur, if you say that again you shall have some brandy and water," so that by the time he was seven the poor child had taken the pledge for life.'

'Gordon drank brandy and soda,' said Harry. 'B and S, he called it. There's a school of thought which holds that he had occasional drinking bouts, hidden away in his tent, a flag and a cutlass crossed on the ground outside to indicate that he shouldn't be disturbed — and after a few days he'd come out, refreshed.'

'You couldn't blame him,' said Jessica.

'I wouldn't,' said Harry. 'His contemporaries tried to play it down, the iconoclasts make much of it, but it seems to me a matter of little importance . . .'

'Do you mind if I sit here?' asked Ronald. 'There are some people smoking at the bar.'

'No, *do* join us,' said Jessica. There would be no room for a fourth person round the small table so close to the window. 'I was just telling Harry,' she said, 'about a woman who gave a child tartar emetic in his wine to put him off drink.'

'Aversion therapy,' said Ronald. 'She belonged to the Behaviourist camp. They try it on homosexuals too. It doesn't work,' he added, his tone disapproving.

'There are those who hold that Gordon was homosexual,' said Harry. 'Chiefly because he never married . . .'

'I'd never have married myself,' said Jessica, 'if I'd *known* . . .'

'Then he took a lot of interest in ragged boys,' said Harry.

'But he also took a lot of interest in the derelict old, and no one has so far accused him of perversion in that respect.'

'Attitudes change so,' said Jessica. 'Look at Helen Huntingdon. Although a lot of people *still* seem to think she was an admirable character – they think she was an early women's libber or something.'

Ronald's attention had been drawn by the word 'perversion'. 'I've been reminding myself of the theories of Krafft-Ebing,' he said. 'Reading up on *Psychopathia Sexualis*. There was a case in 1892, a man called Ardisson – belonged to a family of criminals and insane – small man with a protruding jaw. He used to dig up corpses and . . .'

'Eat them?' asked Harry, suddenly back in the horrors of Khartoum.

'No,' said Ronald. 'He used to . . .' he stopped, remembering again that he was not in his consulting room, and there was a lady present.

'Why did he do that?' asked the lady, who understood perfectly from Ronald's omissions what the small man with the protruding jaw had done.

'If we knew,' said Ronald moodily, 'we'd know more about the mainsprings of human behaviour than we do.' He was sometimes tempted to say, with the rest of the population, that some people were just plain crazy, and leave it at that.

Harry, belatedly catching up with the conversation, remembered the surprising passage in Herodotus where it is revealed that, in ancient Egypt, when a beautiful or well-connected lady died her body was kept some days, until she was past her prime, before it was delivered to the embalmer, since one of the practitioners of this craft had been discovered in carnal intercourse with an attractive corpse and been denounced by a work-mate.

'Yuk,' said Jessica. What an odd conversation for Christmas Eve – but then she was ignoring Christmas, so tonight was no different from any other.

Eric came to collect the glasses from their table and looked at his watch. Finlay's sister-in-law had promised to come in at nine to give him a hand. It was one minute to. As he looked up he saw her behind the bar pulling a pint for Finlay who stood in front of it swaying a little.

'She's an odd-looking woman,' said Anita to no one in particular and unaware of the relationship of the boatman, who stood beside her, to the barmaid. She had noticed for the first time that the barmaid had webbed hands: a thin membrane stretched almost to the second joint of each finger, facilitating the management of the heap of loose change which Finlay offered her.

'She's a selkie,' said Finlay.

'A what?' asked Anita, but Finlay only laughed.

She edged her way to the corner of the bar counter where Eric stood, polishing glasses. 'What's a selkie?' she demanded of him. She was a little drunk for she had told herself that it was, after all, Christmas Eve.

Eric was annoyed. 'It's just one of their stories,' he said. 'Some nonsense . . .'

'Yes, but *what*?' insisted Anita, her curiosity inflamed by his reticence.

'They say some of the island people are descended from seals . . .'

'. . . and they come ashore,' interpolated Finlay, 'and they take off their skins and they dance on yon strand, and sometimes they wed with the children of men . . .'

He was interrupted by his sister-in-law, who leaned over and gave him a shove in the chest with her webbed hand.

'Ach,' he said, as he spilled a little of his beer, and then he laughed again and wandered unsteadily into the hall where he sat down on the chest beneath the coat rack.

'Then what?' asked Anita, buttonholing Eric.

'Oh, they say if their skins are stolen they can't go back to the water, and that's why some of them are still here,' said

Eric impatiently. 'It's a load of nonsense. Just because some of them have got webbed hands and feet – it's all garbage. My wife . . .' he paused.

'What?' asked Anita. 'What about your wife?'

'Nothing,' said Eric. 'She had to go to the mainland. I'd hoped she'd be here to help out over Christmas. That's all. Finlay's sister-in-law is helping out instead.'

'Oh,' said Anita. She looked round to see where Ronald had gone: this primitive myth would be of interest to a student of the human mind. He was talking to Jessica: he was actually addressing himself to Harry, but as Jessica was also sitting at the table Anita assumed he was talking to her, for was she not famous and glamorous? Her first awe of Jessica had been superseded by common sense as she realized that stars were made of flesh and blood, and this in turn had given way to slight contempt: Anita tended to think of all good-looking women as shallow, and by a natural progression of ideas, since most men seemed to prefer the company of good-looking women, she assumed that most men were also shallow – and foolish. But she was disappointed in Ronald, of whom she had expected better.

'Why don't we all go round to my place?' said Mrs H. 'This is no way to celebrate Christmas Eve.'

Eric could have throttled her. The few locals who had been in the bar had left, and now she was proposing to take away his guests and the other two incomers, leaving the place empty. Worse than that – his advertisement had guaranteed a clean, clear freedom from seasonal distractions and she was threatening to plunge the fugitives into the very atmosphere they had fled. He wished he'd had the foresight to bar her at the onset of Advent. He wished he could sit down and cry.

'I've got to get another crate of tonic water,' he said to Finlay's sister-in-law, and went out into the inn yard telling himself he needed a breath of air. Through the blur of tears, which Eric put down to the atmosphere in the bar, he saw a boy sitting on the low wall. 'Oi,' said Eric, blinking and sounding more aggressive than he had intended, 'what are you doing there?'

The boy was very still and for a moment Eric thought he wasn't going to answer. Then he said, 'I'm waiting for my father.'

Eric was about to say 'Your father's not here,' when a pile of empty crates fell down behind him, so instead he cried, 'What the bloody hell?' and spun round, his heart beating frighteningly fast. He expected to find that somebody too ill-bred to use the gents had come out to relieve himself in the yard, but there was no one there. By the time he had restored the crates into an orderly edifice under the light from the kitchen window, he had forgotten about the boy.

'What's all the noise?' asked Jon, when he returned to the bar.

'What noise?' said Eric shortly. If his inn had the custom it deserved nobody would have noticed a slight crash outside.

'Sounded like the outbreak of war,' said Jon, looking let-down.

Eric knew that look: some people enjoyed riots and commotion. Jon had doubtless hoped that a party of Picts had descended to wreak havoc for his diversion. Mrs H. was the same: she enjoyed nothing more than observing trouble from a safe distance: boats foundering, the mink in the hen-run, breaking relationships, the tattooed ones searching for iron bars to stun whomsoever they might identify as an adversary, anything to add colour to island life.

She was fidgeting on her stool, her anorak half off her shoulders, looking round restively for congenial playmates. In the absence of paramours she had the option of finding somebody to amuse her or going home to her husband, who would probably by now be peeling parsnips. 'Tell you what,' she said, singling out the professor, with whom she had an adolescent, back-of-the-class relationship – they teased each other unkindly while tacitly recognizing that their common status of outcast put them, for better for worse, in the same category – 'Why don't we go to your place? It's nearer.'

Despite his depression Eric watched to see how the professor would respond: he was notoriously loth to pour drink down people's throats, although he had arrived with his car boot full of cans of beer and cheap Rioja from a cut-price establishment in London. Eric knew because Finlay, who knew everything, had told him. 'He'll be having a party,' Finlay had said, and laughed. It looked as though, if he wasn't careful, the party would be tonight.

'Come on,' said Mrs H. 'The spooks walk on Christmas Eve. If we all go together we'll be all right. We'll have to hold hands. Maybe we'll see the ghost in the cottage – he makes everything go cold – doesn't he?' she said to the professor.

There was a rumour that once this chilly phantom had proved so alarming that all the ladies in the vicinity had leapt, for comfort, into the professor's bed. He had not had the chance either to affirm or deny the allegation as no one had ever directly taxed him with it, since, in those matters, frothy speculation is frequently more satisfying than the truth. '*Very* cold,' said the professor, smiling knowingly, for he liked to keep the rumour alive.

Mrs H. would have pursued the topic, but Ronald interrupted. 'If the cottage is by the sea,' he observed, 'it must quite often be cold.'

'It isn't that sort of cold,' said Anita.

'What sort of cold?' asked Ronald. 'How do you know what *sort* of cold is under discussion?'

'Rising damp,' said Eric again.

'Ghostly cold is quite different from other sorts of cold,' said Anita, looking Ronald straight in the eye.

Again he was swift to recognize the warning signs. 'I'm not saying it isn't,' he explained. 'I merely wish to know how you *know*?'

'You just do,' said Anita, indicating by her expression that only a perfect idiot could fail to know. She began to remind him of his wife.

'What I say is,' said Mrs H., 'we'd be silly to waste the chance of seeing the ghost when the time's right. They always come out on Christmas Eve – it's the only night they can talk to you.'

'Why do you want to see it?' asked Ronald.

Most of those present considered that this question required no answer: for one thing there were few people who wouldn't want to see a ghost, and for another seeing the ghost was not Mrs H.'s true motive. She wanted to have a party and not go home. It was obvious.

Anita spoke: having once experienced an uncanny cold she felt herself qualified to state a preference. 'I'd like to see it,' she said.

'Has anybody actually *seen* it?' asked Ronald. 'I thought it was merely a sensation of cold.'

'You see it out of the corner of your eye,' said Mrs H. 'It's very frightening. Isn't it?' She appealed to the professor, who was, after all, the proprietor of the phantom.

'So they say,' said the professor. 'It frightened the girls all right.'

Mrs H. cackled.

'Why do you laugh?' asked Ronald, thinking of a theory which held that mirth was a response to fear, deprivation, all manner of unpleasant things, and therefore a sign of neurosis. A truly well-balanced person would never laugh out loud. He had read that the Red Indian, the well-brought-up Chinaman and Lord Chesterfield had all considered laughter to be a social solecism, characterizing the coarse and the low-born who, it was true, would have had much to deplore in their circumstances and little on the surface to giggle about – which went some way to endorsing the theory. Ronald had tried to explain this to his wife when she had accused him of lacking humour, but she had never taken in what he was saying. He was in two minds about the subject: or rather he felt he was keeping an open mind, since received lay opinion at present considered the lack of a sense of humour to be a drawback, and he was increasingly feeling the need to live in the world as well as in his consulting room. His wife had one day wondered aloud whether he had taken up psychiatry because he was barking mad, or whether daily dealings with the unbalanced had driven him so. Even now the memory stung. He smiled, surprising his whiskers which previously had been disturbed only by those jaw movements attendant upon speaking, masticating or the cleaning of the teeth which they surrounded. 'I suppose it is funny,' he said.

'What's funny?' asked Anita.

'Everything,' said Ronald inadequately, and Anita felt sorry for him because he looked so lost.

'I was laughing at everybody standing round trying to decide whether to go and see the ghost or not,' said Mrs H. untruthfully. 'I think you're all scared.'

'I don't think they're *scared* exactly . . .' began Ronald.

'It's not that I'm scared at all,' said Anita. 'Only it's cold enough out there already, and it was trying to rain earlier. I think I'd rather go to bed.'

'You can't go to bed on Christmas Eve,' said Mrs H.

Jessica was beginning to feel restless. 'Do you want to go to a party?' she asked Harry.

'I think I'll have an early night, he said. 'Tired . . .' He did look tired, Jessica now saw. He was pale. She hoped she hadn't wearied him. 'You go,' he said. 'Young people . . .' She stared at him, suspiciously, and he smiled. 'Comparatively young,' he said, and she was reassured: people on the brink of death seldom felt sufficiently vigorous to tease those who were likely to outlive them.

Anita changed her mind again. 'Let's go,' she said.

'You just said you didn't want to,' said Ronald.

'Well, before that I said I did,' said Anita, 'and I do.'

'I'll run the girls there in the Jag,' said the professor, resigned to parting with some of the contents of his cellar.

'We'll walk,' said Jon, bestirring himself from a sullen daydream in which a woman resembling Jessica begged for his forgiveness: in the daydream she was covered in mud and looking far from her best. 'Come on,' he said to her.

'I've left my coat upstairs,' said Jessica. 'I'll have to go and get it.' She went into the hall and nearly tripped over Finlay, who had abruptly stretched out his legs. He opened his eyes and gazed at her. 'Sorry,' she said.

'Why don't we borrow one of these,' said Anita. 'They've been hanging here for days and nobody's collected them.' She reached out for the dark fur and Finlay rose up and silently but firmly took it away from her, replacing it on the peg.

'I'll get your coat too,' said Jessica, observing this interplay of thoughtlessness and rudeness. 'Is your door unlocked?'

'No,' said Anita, who hated above all things to be humiliated and was briefly wishing that she could condemn Finlay to a lingering death. 'I'll go without.'

'You'll be cold,' said Ronald.

'Not in the car,' said Anita, who was warm with rage and embarrassment.

Mrs H. sidled up to Jessica and whispered in her ear. 'Maybe *he's* got another coat,' she said, indicating, at once, the promiscuous garment which sat on the shoulders of a girl who could have been one of the recent wearers or could just as easily have been a different one, and the professor – the master of the robe. She suppressed a laugh as he turned and looked at her, and made histrionic movements relative to zipping up her anorak.

Jon watched as Jessica squeezed into the back seat of the car, trying to make room for Ronald: she showed a great deal of leg as she did so. It wasn't her fault but Jon thought it was.

★

The professor's cottage was remarkably cold, though not, decided Jessica, for any supernatural reason but because he hadn't lit the fire: it was neatly laid and grimly unwelcoming. He ignited one bar of the Calor gas stove and invited them to retain their coats until the atmosphere warmed up.

'Let's light the fire,' said Mrs H., approaching the grate purposefully.

'Don't be silly,' said the professor, impeding her way. 'What's the point of lighting the fire at this time?'

'It would be warmer,' said Mrs H.

'If you want to come down first thing in the morning and clean it out and lay it again then go ahead,' said the professor.

'OK,' said Mrs H., 'where're the matches?'

The professor lost his temper. 'If you're going to take charge,' he said, 'just carry on. You open a bottle – or better still, go back to your place and open your own bottles.'

'Temper, temper,' said Mrs H. She would have persisted and struck a match, but looking round she couldn't see any.

Ronald regarded this display with moderate professional interest. The man was clearly obsessional: people of loose morals were often neurotically economical in other ways. He was quite sure that if the professor saw a pin he would pick it up and conserve it until it came in useful. 'What do you do with your empty cans and old newspapers?' he asked.

'What?' said the professor, controlling himself.

'You must have a lovely view here in the daytime,' said Anita, peering through the window into the murk.

'The cold ghost happened in the summer,' said Mrs H. whose vaguely proprietorial attitude had not been modified by her host's outburst, 'so it was more noticeable.'

Jessica wondered for a moment how she knew so much about it and concluded that she and the professor must once have been closer than they now appeared to be. It was unusual, she thought, for lecherous people to care for each other: they mostly preferred to debauch the virtuous.

'How's the fence holding up?' asked Mrs H. spitefully.

The subject of the fence was a sore spot with the professor: somebody kept pulling it down. Every time he arrived on the island he put it up, and every time somebody came along and pulled it down and danced on his lawn, or so it would appear. The grass would be flattened and parts of the lawn balded, the nasturtiums which trailed the edges thrust carelessly aside. It fronted the sea and was intended to deter tourists from presuming that the professor's garden was a public place suitable for picnics. The odd thing was that even out of the tourist season somebody came along and pulled it down. He had suspected each of the locals in turn, but had no evidence with which to back an accusation and had to content himself with casting unfriendly glances and making veiled remarks, which did little to enhance his popularity.

'I'm going to get Finlay to put it up this time,' he said. 'I'm fed up with hammering in stakes.'

'He'll charge you,' said Mrs H., surprised at this evidence of extravagance.

'He owes me,' said the professor. 'I lent him my outboard-motor last month.'

'It's funny,' said Mrs H., 'considering the amount of time Finlay spends along the shore that he hasn't caught somebody at it.'

'You don't imagine Finlay pushes it over,' said the professor. Finlay was about the only islander he hadn't suspected.

'Why not Finlay?' asked Mrs H. 'Why shouldn't it be him? He's always down there.'

'Why should he?' said the professor.

'Why not?' said Mrs H.

'Don't be ridiculous,' said the professor, who would have found it inconvenient if Finlay should prove to be the culprit, for when his own outboard-motor broke down he often borrowed Finlay's.

★

Jon, walking as rapidly as he could through the night without falling over, came to the kitchen door and stalked in. Jessica was glad to see him since new blood might help to dilute the bad blood presently pulsing through people's veins: if it went on blood might be spilled. 'Isn't this nice?' she said.

'It reminds me of my grandfather's place in Ireland,' said Jon. 'He has a little place like this that he keeps for the fishing and sailing.' This might have been true, but when people had been with Jon for any length of time they ceased to believe a single word he said. If he claimed to have a nose, mouth and ears they would disregard the evidence of their senses and automatically assume that, in one way or another, he must be exaggerating.

'Come and sit by me,' said Jessica, again feeling sorry for him. She patted the worn cloth of the sofa and moved up to make room.

'Well, would anyone like a drink?' asked the professor. He sounded as though he hoped that, with any luck, they might decline.

'I'd love one,' said Jessica firmly.

'Get some glasses,' said the professor to the girl in the duffel coat. 'They're in the bottom cupboard in the kitchen.'

She returned with an assortment of receptacles, none of which matched. Jessica supposed it didn't matter, but it was indicative of the mean-spiritedness that distinguished the evening and she asked herself what she thought she was doing, sitting in a clammy cottage on Christmas Eve with a bunch of people she didn't know. A stiff scotch would go some way to improving matters.

'Beer or wine?' demanded the professor.

'Wine, I guess,' said Jessica resignedly.

'Bring a bottle from the scullery,' said the professor to the girl. 'It's through that door and on the left.' It seemed that she was not altogether familiar with the premises, and Jessica began to reflect on the other women the professor was credited with. Perhaps they were all hanging from hooks in an outhouse like the victims of Mr Fox; perhaps he planned to eat them for lunch next day . . .

'I think I'm homesick,' she said to Jon who was sitting so close she could feel his warmth. She was, indeed, very lost. It was a fault that she was aware of in herself that, in the company of those she found unimportant, her spirits sank: she felt insignificant, plain and ordinary as though ordinariness was contagious. If she wasn't careful she'd start showing off to remind herself that she was quite famous and rich, and could soon be back in the Coach and Horses in Greek Street with all the amusing people she had come here to escape from. She would do this purely for her own benefit and peace of mind and not to impress the others who weren't worth the effort. Jessica was ashamed of her attitude, which made her feel worse.

Jon, though he could not be described as a messenger from the gods, was, at least, a part of the world she was missing. She wished she could ask him when they had met before but she had left it far too late. As the girl pushed a glass of wine into her right hand she found that Jon had taken her left and was fondling it as though he had every right to do so. In order to find a legitimate use for her left hand she demanded of the company if anyone had a cigarette – although she had given up smoking – for she had grown too sympathetic towards him to demand that he unhand her, or to snatch away the member in question with an indignant gesture.

'Oh, no smoking,' said the professor. 'I don't allow smoking here. Anyone who wants to smoke can go outside.' This had the usual effect of inflaming, not only the desire for nicotine, but the urge to swear. All prohibition, when not based on taboo, has a similar consequence. If the professor had requested Jessica to refrain from incest she would have meekly submitted and agreed with his demand: if he had been a bedouin and had forbidden her to use her left hand to pick up a helping of barbecued mutton she would have acquiesced. As it was she determined to get hold of a packet of twenty or die in the attempt.

'I'll have to go back to the inn,' she said. 'I'm gasping for a fag.'

'Try doing without,' said the professor. 'Use some will-power.'

Jessica was accustomed to hearing this phrase on the lips of those who knew her well: it had never had the desired effect on her. 'No,' she said.

'I'll come with you,' said Jon.

'You don't need to,' said Jessica. 'I can see my way.'

'You never know who's around in the night,' said Jon. 'It could be dangerous.'

Jessica thought that walking in the dark with a man who had designs on you was, statistically, more dangerous than walking alone with the off-chance that a stray sex-maniac might leap from behind a hedge and do you a mischief, but she didn't say so.

'Hurry back,' said the professor.

'I have no intention of going back,' said Jessica as they went through the gate. 'Have you?'

'Of course not,' said Jon, who had instantly assumed, and was now convinced, that Jessica was leaving, not in search of cigarettes, but in order to be alone with him.

'Listen,' she said when they had gone a little way along the road, 'I can hear singing.'

'Probably the locals,' said Jon. 'Probably drunk.'

'No, sshh,' said Jessica, standing still. 'Listen a minute.'

'I can only hear the sea,' said Jon, taking the opportunity to put both arms round Jessica as they stood on the dark road.

'If we go on standing here and they *are* drunk,' said Jessica, 'we'll get mown down as they drive home. Come on, I'm freezing again.'

The bar was empty except for Eric who had settled down to drinking a small proportion of the profits, but was, nevertheless, feeling unhappily sober.

'Have you got twenty Silk Cut?' asked Jessica, sitting on a stool and shrugging her coat off. 'The professor wouldn't let me smoke.'

'He wouldn't,' said Eric.

'What's he a professor of?' asked Jessica who had, intermittently, wondered about this for some time. He didn't strike her as being cast in the donnish mould.

'Teeth,' said Eric contemptuously. 'He's a dentist.'

'Ah,' said Jessica. 'How revolting.'

'He makes a fortune in one way and another,' said Eric, 'and he gets months of holiday.'

There followed one of those satisfying discussions, in which all parties are in agreement, about the iniquities of the medical and dental professions and the shortcomings of the NHS, leavened by individual accounts of appalling experiences, both surgical and financial, which each participant had undergone at the hands of one or more practitioners of these humane skills.

'They call him the gas-poker,' said Eric indiscreetly. He tried, most of the time, to be the ideal innkeeper, never discussing the idiosyncrasies of the clients, and certainly never while presiding in his own professional capacity in his bar, but misery and whisky made him bitter and loosened his tongue. 'Nothing's ever been proved, but they say he takes advantage of his patients. I don't really believe he's a professor at all. I think they just call him that. I think he's a common-or-garden tooth-puller.'

'Give me a large whisky and ginger,' said Jessica, 'and I'll go back and ask him.'

'Why?' asked Jon.

'Because I want to know,' said Jessica. 'I'm curious.'

'It seems terribly boring to me,' said Jon. 'Who cares what he is?'

'I don't precisely *care*,' explained Jessica, 'I'd simply like to know for my own satisfaction.' She glared at Jon, thinking that he was accusing her of being nosey, and not realizing that he was seized in the throes of jealousy at hearing her express interest in their erstwhile host.

'That cottage is the most uncomfortable dump I've ever been in,' said Jon.

'I thought it reminded you of your grandfather's place,' said Jessica vengefully.

'Only its position,' said Jon, 'only the way it stands by the edge of the sea. My grandfather's place is furnished with family heirlooms and there are huge log fires.'

'I thought they burned peat in Ireland,' said Jessica and immediately regretted it. She was annoyed with Jon but not sufficiently annoyed to question his fantasies. She didn't care enough.

'They bring in logs from the estate,' said Jon.

'Oh,' said Jessica. She changed the subject. 'Where's the barmaid?' she inquired of Eric.

'I let her go home,' said Eric. 'She's coming in early tomorrow to help.'

'How lucky you are to have found staff,' said Jessica, who believed, correctly, that it was growing increasingly difficult to persuade anyone to work for a living.

'You're right,' said Eric. 'I don't know what I'd do without her . . .' He paused, not wanting to give an impression of insecurity, of near desperation.

'I don't suppose you'll have to,' said Jessica, comfortingly. 'She looks very content with her lot.'

Jon found this conversation about the work force tedious in the extreme since it had no relevance to himself and did nothing to further his relationship with Jessica. He could think of no satisfactory way to wrench her from the bar: he didn't want to go back to the cottage and he was sufficiently clear-sighted to realize that he couldn't suggest they go up to her room. He was baffled by her behaviour.

'I think I'll go to bed,' said Jessica, deciding against returning to the cottage to interrogate the professor on his vocation.

Jon smiled.

The atmosphere in the cottage was slowly warming up. Two more girls had arrived and had insisted on opening another bottle of wine and turning on the second bar of the Calor heater. They both seemed to know the professor quite well and to be familiar with his ways.

'And what do you do?' asked one, seating herself beside Ronald.

'I'm a psychoanalyst,' said Ronald, unwarily. He wondered if he'd ever learn.

'I might have known,' said the girl, delighted. 'You look like one of them.' She patted his beard. 'Tell me about myself. What's wrong with me?'

'You haven't got any manners,' said Ronald, averting his beard from her affectionate fingers. This was the sort of female he couldn't stand.

She laughed, even more delighted. 'How do you know?' she asked. 'How can you tell? Let's go into the other room and you can tell me all about me.'

'He doesn't give free consultations,' said Anita. The girl eyed her, up and down, unsmiling and then disregarded her. Anita moved closer to Ronald on his other side.

'Come on,' said the girl. 'I need some help. I keep falling in love with the wrong men.'

'How unfortunate for you,' said Anita.

'I don't have any trouble finding them,' said the girl, 'only keeping them.'

Ronald found this totally unsurprising. 'I can give you the name of a good man in Edinburgh,' he said, which was untrue but was his usual method of coping with this type of thing when he had his wits about him.

'I wouldn't mind having the name of a good man anywhere,' said the girl, and shrieked with merriment. She was the worst girl Ronald had seen for some time.

'Ronald,' said Anita, in a confidential undertone, 'you know I met this woman who knits special sweaters. Do you remember? Well, I know tomorrow's Christmas day, but I want to go and find her again before we go home, so will you come with me?' This was the only claim to his attention that she could think of on the spur of the moment.

'What time?' asked Ronald.

'I don't know what time,' said Anita exasperatedly. A literal response to a ruse is both disconcerting and infuriating and does nothing to advance matters. 'Any time. Before lunch or after.'

'All right,' said Ronald.

'Thanks,' said Anita. 'Thanks very much.'

Ronald understood from this that she was angry with him and was conscious of a renewed interest in her. He thought detachedly of one of Krafft-Ebing's case histories. *Z, who had noticed that females, no matter how ugly, always excited him sexually when he discovered anything domineering in their character. An angry word from the lips of such a woman was sufficient to give him the most violent erections. Thus, one day he was sitting in a café when he heard the (ugly) female cashier scold the waiters in a loud voice, which threw him into the most intense sexual excitement which soon induced ejaculation.* In fairness to himself Ronald acknowledged that he was not precisely similar to the unfortunate, or possibly fortunate, Z, but he decided to have another look at the romances of Sacher-Masoch and reacquaint himself with the various theories arising therefrom.

'You don't have to come if you don't want to,' said Anita, who was about to relapse into a sulk.

'I do,' said Ronald tenderly, 'I do want to.'

She turned to look at him in surprise, thinking that she'd

113

never understand men, and then her gaze went past him to the window and she yelped.

'What's wrong?' asked the professor, startled.

'There's somebody at the window,' said Anita. 'I saw somebody staring in.'

'It'll only be one of the girls,' said the professor serenely. The door blew open on a gust of wind and the flames in the Calor heater flared. 'There,' he said, 'she'll be coming in now,' but nobody appeared. 'Funny,' he said, getting up and closing the door. 'She must've thought better of it when she saw us all here.'

'It didn't look like a girl,' said Anita. 'It looked like a boy.'

'A lot of my girls look like boys,' said the professor, with the same serenity, and Ronald regarded him, his professional interest again aroused.

'Brrr,' said a girl, 'it's freezing in here. I wonder who the silly cow was. She's let in the draught.'

'Don't be rude about her,' said the professor, with one of his smiles. 'She's probably shy.'

'It was a boy . . .' began Anita.

'One of my adoring women,' said the professor, giving rise to a scene as two of the girls fell upon him to reward his conceit by pulling his hair and disarranging his clothing. The third girl observed them sullenly and then went out, to return with another bottle of wine which she proceeded to open, pour into a tumbler and drink.

'Hey,' said the professor, struggling up from his chair at this evidence of profligacy.

'Get knotted,' said the girl, retreating with both glass and bottle.

'I think it's time we went home,' said Anita, standing up and putting her glass down. 'Thank you for a lovely evening.' She put her arm through Ronald's as they reached the road. 'He's a vulgar man,' she observed.

'He has pronounced homosexual tendencies,' said Ronald.

'Has he?' said Anita. 'How do you know?' She wondered if the professor, unnoticed, had pressed his attentions on Ronald.

'I've had patients like him,' said Ronald.

'Or is it because his girls look like boys?' asked Anita, inspired.

'Not necessarily,' said Ronald. 'No, it is merely that I have had several patients who have manifested a similar behaviour pattern, and when I have observed them over a sufficient period of time, have gained their confidence and probed sufficiently profoundly into their unconscious processes . . .'

'. . . they've turned out to be queer as coots,' supplied Anita, translating what she guessed he was about to say into a more comprehensible form, partly to illustrate that she was familiar with the vernacular and partly as a gentle snub.

'Yes,' said Ronald, gratified by her ready comprehension, and unperturbed by her manner of expressing herself. They walked slowly, in accord.

'We didn't even see a ghost,' said Anita, pressing closer to her companion.

Harry sat alone in his room long after midnight had passed, trying to make sense of his sorrow. He knew that if you lived long enough you would inevitably, to a greater or lesser extent, become disenchanted with everybody in your life, from your nearest and dearest right down to the amiable newsagent on the corner. All the people in the inn were in the throes of disappointment: that was why they were here. How fortunate they were, thought Harry. How strangely blessed to have learned that love is illusion, to have been given time to see its blossoms moulder and spot and not to have had it snatched away from them in perfection. He told himself that if his wife had lived she might now be a false-toothed harridan, sitting up in the bed behind him demanding to know what he thought he was doing staring out of the window like that. His son, if he had lived, might now be a pompous middle-aged man with a plump-wristed wife of his own and a tendency to gout. How peaceful that would be, thought Harry; how painless to have learned to the full that love withers and nothing matters. How pleasant to have realized completely the tedium of life and to have no fear of loss and no pangs of remembrance. That would be the consolation of age, and he had no such solace, for his wife and child had gone in beauty and youth, cheated him of disillusion and left him endlessly bereft. Perhaps it was perversity that had kept him from remarrying, a determination to mourn without distraction. It had seemed at the time like integrity, and indeed, a second wife would have devalued the first — that was undeniable — but that very betrayal would have eased the cold and barren purity of his heart: infidelities, what are known as 'small human weaknesses', by their corrupting processes warmed a man, blurring his perceptions, negating his strength and — permitting him to roll round in the midden — thought Harry, suddenly impatient with all this self-pity. It was nearly two of the clock on Christmas morning.

'Psst,' came a whisper at the door. 'I'm sorry,' said Jessica when he opened it, 'but I saw your light was on . . .'

'Come in,' said Harry, relieved at any distraction. She closed the door behind her.

'Can't you sleep either?' asked Harry.

'That's just it,' said Jessica. 'I could, easily, but that boy has gone completely mad and I can't.'

'What's he doing?' inquired Harry, indicating that she should sit in the armchair.

Jessica sat back. 'He's not *doing* anything,' she said, 'not really. That's what's so peculiar. We got back from the professor's — and he's pretty peculiar too, I can tell you — and I said good night and went up to bed and Jon followed me and I couldn't quite screech like a maiden, "Get out of my chamber, you brute," so I waited, and he took his sweater off, and then he took his shirt off, and he was watching me all the time and smiling. And then I said I'd go and get a bottle from the bar, and here I am.'

'I see,' said Harry.

'I don't,' said Jessica. 'I'm damned if I do. He was perform-ing a strip-tease – like a girl. That's what he was doing. He was looking at me under his eyelashes and exposing his torso, and any minute we'd've been down to the suspender-belt and the fishnets, in a manner of speaking, and I was meant to be going *Cor*, like the audience at Fifi la Frou-Frou's, and, all in all, I missed my cue.'

'Are you all right?' asked Harry.

'I'm fine,' said Jessica. 'Except I don't understand what's going on. A straightforward pass I understand, but this is different again. Creepy. What would *you* think if I started twirling my moustaches at you?'

'I'd be very surprised,' said Harry.

'Exactly,' said Jessica. 'Can we blame the women's libera-tion movement, do you think? Are we into total role-reversal?'

'Perhaps,' said Harry.

'I mean – I don't wish to sound offensive, but except under special circumstances the male form is not a pretty sight – I mean if somebody cuts out all the preliminaries and simply flings himself at you in his pelt, you think, well, forget the whole thing. Not that he flung. I think he was expecting *me* to fling.'

'I can quite see that,' said Harry, referring to the earlier part of her remark.

'They never used to do it,' said Jessica, puzzling away at the infinite perplexities of life. 'What shall I do now? What can I say to him? If he'd made a pass at me I'd know, but as it is we have no clear basis for discussion. Shall I say, "Get 'em on," and hurl him bodily from my room?'

'Do you want me to come with you?' asked Harry.

'No,' said Jessica. 'It would be too embarrassing. I can't stand scenes off-stage. And he hasn't really done anything. He's perfectly harmless really . . .' although even as she said it she was aware of a certain uneasiness. She construed it as misplaced compassion. 'Poor little sod,' she said. 'Can I stay here a bit longer until he gets fed up waiting?'

'Of course,' said Harry. 'Shall I make some tea? Coffee?'

'I'll do it,' said Jessica, thinking of people who led ordinary lives, who would now be putting the last touches to the Christmas tree, checking on the brandy butter, worrying about the debt they'd plunged themselves into, creeping into the children's bedrooms on one stockinged foot, while in the stocking which would have clad the other foot were crammed toy cars, small representations of appealing aliens, jigsaw puzzles, picture-books, a tangerine and a nut – or perhaps some of them were creeping for the purposes of child abuse. 'I have a sense of evil,' she said, 'of something out of place . . .'

'The man in your room?' suggested Harry.

'I don't think it's just that,' said Jessica. 'I'm more or less used to that sort of thing. It's not my springtime innocence I fear for. It's more a sense of emptiness, of no hope. I guess I've been drinking too much recently. In the end it just makes you sad. I'm sad.'

'What do you usually do on Christmas Eve?' asked Harry.

'Get drunk, I suppose,' said Jessica. 'Go to Brompton Oratory for midnight mass with a crowd of people. Get drunk again. Nothing much.' She poured boiling water on to the tea-bags and opened a plastic container of milk with her thumb-nail. 'Milk?' she inquired.

'No, thank you,' said Harry.

'I'm sorry to be so depressing,' said Jessica. 'I'm not usually – I think,' she added modestly. 'Except for you I don't much like the people here. Maybe that's it. Maybe this whole idea was a huge mistake. It was bound to be when you come to think about it – plunging yourself into a load of strangers at the edge of the world. Trouble is – when you get there you find it isn't the edge of the world. I think I forgot the world is round, so no matter where you go, no matter how far you run, sooner or later you find yourself staring at your own retreating backside. How pointless everything is.'

Harry had no words of comfort. He would have said that the pointlessness existed because she had left Christ out of Christmas. She had had sufficient good sense and good taste to learn to eschew the bacchanalian excesses of the season, but not enough to realize what else she had sacrificed. You could say, thought Harry, that she had thrown out the Holy Child with the bath salts, bath oil, bath essence and bubbles which so often appeared as gifts, unknowingly symbolizing the frankincense and myrrh . . .

'What are you thinking about?' asked Jessica and wished she hadn't, because he might well have been remembering Christmasses past when he would now have been watching the look of delight on the face of his little son as he woke to a snowy morning and a glowing fire in the dawn and a new train set, and cream on his porridge instead of milk, as a special treat . . . sentimental tears began to slide down her make-up.

'Don't cry,' said Harry.

'I'm so sorry,' said Jessica. 'Men hate tears.'

'I don't mind,' said Harry. 'I don't like to see you upset.' He would have told her that he himself sometimes wept, but he knew that women cannot bear to see men weep. 'How about a brandy?'

'And soda?' said Jessica, attempting to substitute a smile for a snivel. 'Drink to General Gordon?'

'Why not?' said Harry. 'He was an amazing fellow for looking on the bright side.'

'I suppose he'd need to be,' said Jessica. 'Stuck in Khartoum like that. I've nearly gone mad stuck on Crewe platform for an hour – and nobody was proposing to massacre me.'

'I know something to cheer you up,' said Harry. 'I'll read you some last words.'

'Thanks a lot,' said Jessica, drying her tears.

'Now where is it . . .' said Harry. 'Here we are, this is about Achmet Pasha Said — he was the Turkish commandant of El Obeid and he refused to surrender to the Mahdi. It comes from the account of Father Bononi, who was a Catholic priest besieged in the garrison. "On the 18th January in 1883 the dervishes entered the dewan of the Mudiriah and found Achmet Pasha Said sitting in a high, carved, armed-chair of stained wood, bolt upright, with his arms folded, staring at them defiantly." They were going to kill him, but some of them said he must be taken before the Mahdi. Listen: "'Back dogs; touch me not,' he cried. 'You defile me, base rebels. I will go myself before this arch rebel Mohammed Ahmed. Lead on.' They instinctively drew back, startled at his terrible voice and fierce aspect. 'Hold his hands and search him,' ordered Mohammed Ahmed the moment he saw him; and he was just in time with this precaution. The old man was drawing forth from his breast a revolver, and undoubtedly meant to deal death to his enemy. 'Take the cursed dog of a Turk away,' cried Mohammed Ahmed, 'and sell him for a slave by auction in the bazaar. Away with him.' Then was the commandant led forth and exposed for sale, but no man durst buy him at first. But it happened that an Emir passed by that way, and out of derision cried out, 'O auctioneer, I will surely give 680 piastres for this man.' So he was knocked down to the Emir. Now, when this came to the ears of Mohammed Ahmed he sent forth an order that the commandant should be slain with all speed. So some dervishes went from the Mahdi's presence then and there and sought out the commandant. They heard he was in the house of the Emir; they went there and ordered that Achmet Pasha should be brought forth. He presented himself to them with unquailing look and bold bearing as the dervishes drew their swords.

'You have come to murder me, have you? Cursed, cowardly dogs, I fear you not. May your fathers' graves be defiled. I curse them, you and the foul harlots that bore you. I curse your fathers and mothers back to three generations. All your female relations are abandoned women, and may the graves of your forefathers be defiled. I curse you all.' They fell upon him pouring forth these maledictions, and he died like a brave man, with the utmost fortitude." What do you think of that?' asked Harry, laying aside the book.

Jessica said that, yes indeed, and oddly enough, she had found it cheering; that, when you came to think about it, perhaps ultimate bravery was the foremost and most valuable of all human qualities; and furthermore that, given our circumstances, it was, in the end, the only *necessary* virtue. 'What happened next?' she asked.

'Bloodshed, mayhem,' said Harry. 'These are strange tales to be telling on Christmas morning.'

'Go on,' said Jessica.

'Really?' said Harry.

'Oh yes,' said Jessica.

'This is Father Bononi again,' said Harry. ' "I forgot to mention that on the entering of the town by the dervishes this gallant soldier . . ." that's Achmet Pasha, ". . . tried to blow up the magazine and destroy himself and army with the rebels, but the officers prevented him. The dervishes now in their rage – for they were cut to the quick by the words of the commandant – sought out Ali Bey Sherif; him they also slew with other officers. Now the dervishes returned to Mohammed Ahmed, and told all of these things to him. He burst into a flood of tears, threw dust on his head, and upbraided them for thus spilling blood: 'Ye be sanguinary men, O ye dervishes. These deeds do not find favour in my sight.' " '

'That's a bit rich,' said Jessica, after a moment's silence.

'The Mahdi, too, was a complex man,' said Harry.

'What happened to him?' asked Jessica.

'He died of smallpox in 1885,' said Harry.

'It all makes everything look a bit of a waste of time,' said Jessica. 'Time, and blood, and everything.'

'Not a waste of time,' said Harry. 'Life is only, by definition, a use of time. That's all it was ever meant to be. We only waste it if we try too hard to make sense of it. I know . . .'

'What do you know?' asked Jessica.

'Just how much time you can waste,' said Harry, 'when you have no purpose for it, except to try and make sense of it.'

Jessica thought she must be growing tired, for she could not understand him.

'I'll come with you to your room,' he said, 'and look under the bed.'

The room was empty and cold, for the window was wide open.

'What's all that about?' said Jessica, crossing the room and leaning out over the sill to look down to the sea. 'Do you think he shinned down the drainpipe, or did he open the window to annoy me? Maybe he means to climb in again?'

'Let me,' said Harry. He closed the window and drew the curtains across. 'Lock your door and go to sleep,' he said. 'You've had a long night.'

'Good night,' said Jessica, and she yawned.

Before dawn she woke, half dreaming that she could hear the sound of movement outside. The smell of the sea was strong in the room and she remembered the open window and blamed Jon. Not quite awake she went to check that the window was still closed, drew the curtains and looked out: all she could see was mist, paler than the dying night, drifting formlessly over the shore. 'Merry Christmas,' she said to herself and went back to bed.

Descending to the dining room before nine she found it

deserted except for Finlay, who was lighting the fire. Here, too, there was a strong smell of the sea: it must emanate from Finlay, decided Jessica. He had probably been up since day-break gutting mackerel, tying lobsters' claws together, boiling shrimps and crimping salmon – oh shut up, Jessica – she told herself. 'Morning,' she said aloud.

'Aye,' said Finlay, agreeing with this proposition.

'Nice day,' said Jessica, since it seemed not to be raining.

'Aye,' said Finlay equably.

'No sign of snow,' said Jessica.

'No,' said Finlay.

'Where is everyone?' asked Jessica, wishing she'd told him that he had a frog in his hair and wondering how he would have responded.

'They're no' up yet,' explained Finlay, and although she knew this to be the most likely explanation for their absence Jessica had again the irrational fear of the child who suspects itself to have been abandoned. I must have had a lousy upbringing she thought, perhaps I should consult Ronald about it.

Finlay's sister-in-law came in from the kitchen and regarded her inquiringly.

'Haddock,' said Jessica recklessly, 'haddock with a poached egg on, and toast.'

She moved away from the fire: if she got too warm and also ate a full breakfast she would fall asleep in her chair and wake up looking fat-faced and ugly. Already she was looking plain, as she had ascertained from the mirror in the bathroom; a candid, even cruel mirror with a tendency to distort the features width-wise.

Anita came in with silver droplets in her hair. 'I've been for a walk,' she said. 'It's almost like spring.'

'No, it isn't,' said Jessica, looking at the window. 'It's all grey and horrible.'

'It's got quite warm,' said Anita. 'It doesn't feel cold at all this morning. The snow's all gone from the hilltop.'

'How *depressing*,' said Jessica.

This put Anita in a difficult position: she, too, regretted the melting of the snow, but if she had said so she would have seemed to be complaining, and she meant to be optimistic and cheerful for, no matter what everyone said, today was Christmas day after all. 'It's quite pleasant,' she said.

'Well, I'll come for a walk with you later,' said Jessica. 'I'm having haddock for breakfast, so it can go down and beat the hell out of the alcohol in my system, and then I'll have to go and walk it off or it's going to lock the doors against lunch.'

'I shall have grapefruit,' said Anita, who was beginning to manifest, by the day, a greater independence of spirit than she had shown in the store, subjected, as she had been, to the tyrannical whims of a higher authority.

'It's nasty,' said Jessica gloomily. 'Little and dry and sour, and all its vitamins have fallen out.'

'It isn't fattening,' said Anita.

'It isn't *anything*,' said Jessica: she stopped talking as Eric came in with the haddock.

'Hot rolls?' he offered. 'They've just come out of the oven.'

'I mustn't eat hot rolls,' said Jessica. 'I shouldn't eat anything really. I think I've put on a stone.'

'Not at all,' said Eric, annoyed. If the inn food was so delicious that she couldn't resist it she should not be complaining, but congratulating him.

Jessica, too, realized this. 'Everything is so *delicious*,' she explained.

'We do our best to give satisfaction,' said Eric, mollified. He had been up for a long time, putting things to rights before he had started agitating himself about his culinary arrangements for the day. There had been a number of dead fish in the inn yard, flung up by some freak wave or gust of wind, and he had had to shovel them up and dispose of them: he had decided against putting them in the bins and had eventually carried them in the log-basket and thrown them back into the sea. The log-basket still smelled fishy, but the inn was on the edge of the ocean and people must be prepared for an oceanic atmosphere; it could be regarded as an added attraction.

Jessica did not so regard it: she had eaten her haddock, and when Finlay's sister-in-law had leaned over her to remove her plate with its bones and skin she had been nearly overwhelmed by the odour of fish. The whole family must have been wallowing in the things all night, she thought. Perhaps they were running a canning industry on the side, or perhaps they never washed. 'I feel sick,' she said. 'Tired,' she added, as Eric was within earshot. 'I think I'll go and lie down.'

'What about your walk?' asked Anita.

'Bother my walk,' said Jessica. 'I'll go later.' And she went back to bed, so that when Jon came into the dining room he saw no sign of her.

'Good morning,' said Anita.

'Good morning,' said Jon with a smile that he had last used in a commercial for tinned soup, when his supposed mother had placed before him a plate of supposed minestrone: it was the sort of smile that the Elect might wear for the Second Coming, and Anita was considerably disconcerted by it. She looked round to see at whom it might be directed and narrowed her eyes when she realized it could only be herself. What's *his* game? she surmised suspiciously.

Ronald also caught the afterglow of this smile, and inwardly deplored it. He shook his head as he took his place at the table.

'What's wrong?' asked Anita solicitously. 'Do you have a headache?' Ronald thought about it: he hadn't noticed it before but now he was conscious of a mild discomfort in the top of his head.

'Yes,' he said. 'I think I have.'

'I've got a paracetamol in here,' said Anita, grasping her handbag. 'Drink it with a lot of water and you'll feel better.'

Since she had perceived Ronald as a little boy she had grown to disregard his medical qualifications. Ronald did as he was bid.

'You are a very sensible woman,' he said, which had she but known it was the highest praise he could offer. She would have preferred to be described as a 'proper' woman: she sometimes dreamed that someone would so categorize her. 'Now take Anita,' they'd say, 'there's a proper woman.'

'I think that wine was off,' she said. 'I felt rather bad in the night. I had to get up. What happened to you?' she said to Jon. 'Why didn't you come back?'

'Because the wine was off,' said Jon, idly unoriginal since his mind was elsewhere.

'You didn't miss much,' said Anita. 'We came back soon after you. There was quite an unpleasant scene developing.'

'Oh, yeah?' said Jon, who had no interest in other people's scenes, pleasant or unpleasant.

'Have you got a headache too?' asked Anita sharply as she noticed the expression which had moved in to replace the smile.

Jon recalled himself. 'Me? No,' he said. 'No, no, I'm fine,' and he smiled again and stretched out his arms in his lazy panther style.

If Jon had been his patient, thought Ronald, he would now be hurriedly consulting a colleague as to the immediate necessity of having him sectioned. 'Do you ever hear voices?' he asked, but Jon, now dreamily smiling, had lowered his arms and left the room.

'Why did you ask him that?' demanded Anita.

'He's mad,' said Ronald, putting it in the simplest terms for the layman: he was prepared to trust Anita with a few professional confidences.

'What sort of mad?' asked Anita.

'Paranoiac,' said Ronald, reaching for a roll. 'Where's my breakfast?'

'You mean he thinks people are getting at him?' persisted Anita.

'I think I'll have kippers,' said Ronald. 'What . . .?'

'Do you mean he thinks people are trying to kill him?' said Anita.

'Not necessarily,' said Ronald. 'It's more complicated than that.' He was not prepared to go into the complexities of paranoiac hallucination, of persecution dread and omnipotent fantasy.

'Is he dangerous?' demanded Anita.

'Probably,' said Ronald.

'But . . .' said Anita.

'I'm so hungry,' said Ronald pathetically. 'Where's my kipper?'

Anita stood up and went to the kitchen door. 'Could we have a kipper here?' she asked sweetly and politely. Ronald found her lovely, seeking food for him.

'Sorry,' said Eric, panting slightly. 'I didn't realize you were down.' The Raeburn had chosen this morning to start playing up. 'Pair of kippers just coming.'

'But what might he do?' said Anita.

'Who?' asked Ronald.

'*Jon*,' said Anita. 'What might he *do*?'

'I've no idea,' said Ronald. 'He might do anything.'

'Yes, but *what*?' asked Anita, her voice rising.

Finlay's sister-in-law entered with the kippers.

'I always have trouble with the bones,' said Ronald, 'but I do like a nice kipper.'

'Kippers!' said Harry as he came into the dining room. 'I'm sorry I'm late,' he said to Finlay's sister-in-law. 'I lost track of time. Can I have a kipper?' He sat down opposite Ronald and poured himself a cup of coffee.

'That's a bit cold,' said Anita, resigning herself to abandoning the subject of high mania for the time being. 'I'll ask for some fresh for you.'

Ronald, as he picked a fish bone out of his whiskers, reflected that Anita was that rare being, a proper woman.

'How was your evening?' asked Harry. 'Did you enjoy it?'

'Well, not really,' said Anita. 'Did you, Ronald?'

'Did I what?' asked Ronald, pushing a kipper's eye to the edge of the plate.

'Did you enjoy the evening at the professor's?'

'No, not really,' said Ronald, considering the matter. 'I don't think I did.'

'Oh dear,' said Harry, 'what was wrong?'

Ronald, inartistically splitting the backbone from the flesh of his fish, did not immediately respond.

'It was uncomfortable,' said Anita. 'I don't want to sound ungrateful, but I didn't feel easy there. If you didn't find me silly I'd say there was a feeling of evil about the place . . .'

'Funny you should say that,' said Harry.

'Why?' asked Anita.

'Jessica was saying something similar.'

'Oh,' said Anita, who still had her doubts about Jessica: she found her fanciful.

'What gave you that impression?' asked Harry as his kipper arrived.

Anita waited until Finlay's sister-in-law had gone out again. 'I don't want to sound *fanciful*,' she said, '. . . it's hard to describe. I didn't get any sense of welcome, of friendship . . .' She paused as she strove to find words to illustrate the sense of lovelessness she had felt. She had never been in a brothel but she thought the atmosphere might have been the same.

'It was freezing cold,' said Ronald. 'They wouldn't light the fire.'

Anita was surprised he'd noticed. 'And the wine wasn't very nice,' she said.

'And there wasn't much of it,' said Ronald, surprising her further with this evidence of flawed humanity.

'It's not that we're greedy,' she explained. 'It's the thought.'

'Perhaps it was just as well,' said Harry. 'If you'd drunk too much bad wine you'd be in no condition for today.'

'What time is lunch?' asked Ronald, fishing a final bone from its hiding place behind a molar.

'You can't think about lunch yet,' cried Anita. 'You've hardly finished breakfast.'

'I thought between two and three,' said Eric bearing in another plateful of rolls. 'I don't want to tie you down too closely today, but if anyone's hungry there's always elevenses.' He was still having trouble with the Raeburn. Bloody thing. He had also been overcome by a jealous curiosity as to what his wife might be up to today of all days. It was almost unbearable, and between that anguish and his responsibilities to the guests he thought he might scream, throw back his head, hurl down the plate and howl.

'That'll be fine,' said Anita firmly as Ronald showed signs of speaking. Already she had taken a decision not to allow him to make a spectacle of himself and certainly not today by demanding his lunch at the usual time.

Eric relaxed a little. She wasn't a bad old stick, this guest.

'Do you think the islanders would mind if I called on them today?' asked Anita.

'Do I . . .?' said Eric, bewildered by her unexpected query.

'You say they don't bother about Christmas,' said Anita. 'And as I haven't got much longer here, I thought I'd go and see that lady about the knitting again.'

'Oh yes,' said Eric. 'No, I shouldn't think she'd mind at all.' If he was right in his suppositions the lady would be only too enchanted to get the chance to rip off a mug from the city. 'No, go along and try it out. I'm sure she won't mind.'

'Are you more or less ready, Ronald?' asked Anita.

'What for?' asked Ronald.

'You are coming with me,' explained Anita patiently, 'to

talk to a lady I met, who knits special sweaters with a special pattern so that when her husband and sons get drowned she can identify the bodies.'

'Oh yes, of course,' said Ronald. 'I remember now. I said I'd come, didn't I?'

'Yes,' said Anita. 'You did.'

'I'll go and get my coat,' said Ronald after a short silence, illustrative of some reluctance.

'You can't spend the morning pigging crisps and nuts in the bar,' said Anita on a sudden surge of gaiety.

So that's the way the wind's blowing, thought Eric. For she had sounded quite like a wife in a not unreasonable humour.

'It's me again,' said Jessica when Harry opened the door. 'You are the soul of courtesy and I — I am an unmannerly wretch, and things like that, to take advantage of your good nature.'

'Come in,' said Harry, making his customary allowances for other people's tiresome ways.

'I'm sorry,' said Jessica. 'Sometimes I forget you're not the sort of person . . . oh, never mind.'

'Chair?' invited Harry.

'I mean, I sometimes forget I don't always have to behave the way I imagine people expect actresses to behave,' continued Jessica. 'You'll have to make allowances for me.'

'I do,' said Harry.

'Oh,' said Jessica.

'Is Jon bothering you again?' asked Harry.

'No,' said Jessica. 'He's disappeared. It's something else. I'm frightened of Hell. It's Helen Huntingdon's fault. No it isn't, it's the fault of this island . . .'

'No it isn't,' said Harry.

'Isn't it?' asked Jessica.

'No,' said Harry.

'Why not?' she said. 'Do you mean I'm going off my head?'

'No,' said Harry.

'What do you *mean*?' she asked.

'I don't mean anything much,' said Harry, 'but Hell isn't here and evil doesn't crawl out from the rocks. You could say the island is indifferent but you can't say it's malevolent.'

'It feels it sometimes,' said Jessica.

'I know,' said Harry.

'Maybe it *is* the people,' said Jessica. 'Not so much the islanders, but I get the feeling a number of people come here to do things they wouldn't do in their own back yards – making the place a sort of moral dustbin – if you follow me. Or am I being over-sensitive? Maybe it's only the holiday atmosphere.'

'Tourism always has a corrupting influence,' said Harry. 'Perhaps that's what you're conscious of?'

'I hate everybody today,' said Jessica. 'Everybody is so selfish and self-regarding and I wouldn't mind, except when I see them being like that I'm reminded that I'm the most selfish and self-regarding one of all. I thought if I ignored Christmas it would be all right, but there's always *something*.'

Or nothing, thought Harry, but he said: 'Do you think the antics of Jon have upset you more than you realize?'

'He didn't help,' said Jessica. 'That sort of thing's always depressing, but it isn't only him. Anita's depressing and Ronald's depressing and the dentist – or the professor, or whatever he is – is depressing and Mrs H. reminds me of a rat – I think it's her nose, it twitches – and the weather's depressing and I'm depressing. I wonder if Eric would let me help in the kitchen? I'd like to feel I was of some use to someone. I could make bread – up to my elbows in flour.' She saw herself, rosy-cheeked, wearing a white apron, mingling her skin cells with the sacredness of bread and earning the approbation of God and the angels.

'Are you good at making bread?' asked Harry.

'I never tried,' said Jessica. 'I don't suppose I would be.'

131

'It's quite simple,' said Harry.

Jessica didn't ask him how he knew, because she knew how he knew – they would have made their own bread at a table in the Manse kitchen, and they would have cried to the young Harry: 'Take off your uniform or you'll spoil it, put up your sword, and wash your hands and you can help us make the bread . . .'

She stood up and straightened her skirt. 'I can make cakes,' she said, 'only there's seldom any point.'

'You needn't go,' said Harry. 'I'm not doing anything.'

'It's the oppression,' said Jessica. 'I don't know where to go to get away from the oppression. Don't you feel it?'

'Not the way you do,' said Harry, who was aware only of emptiness, weightless and waiting.

'You're so lucky,' said Jessica without thinking. Anyone who did not feel as she presently did was fortunate.

'Do you want to go down to the bar?' asked Harry.

'I suppose that's all I can do,' said Jessica. 'Though I don't want to end up like Huntingdon. He's got the horrors, and old Helen keeps telling him there's nothing the matter with him except what he brought on himself against her earnest exhortation and entreaty, and then he says if she doesn't shut her trap he's going to order another six bottles of wine and sink the lot. And I don't blame him. I wish I had something else to read. Helen would drive a saint to drink. I expect it's her who's made me feel like this.'

'A brandy and soda will do you little harm,' said Harry.

'Try telling that to Helen Huntingdon,' said Jessica, 'and she'll slip you an ipecacuanha.'

The bar was deserted. 'Tell me some more about Achmet Pasha,' requested Jessica as they stood at the counter. 'He sounds exactly my type.'

'I don't know much more,' said Harry.

'They do that sort of thing in films,' said Jessica. 'When the hero is tied hand and foot in the dentist's chair surrounded by his enemies, who are mostly half-wits, he starts insulting them, which always strikes me as most ill-advised, but apparently what he's trying to do is rattle them so that they make an unwary move. Then the arch villain wastes valuable time boasting about how clever he's been to get the hero into the dentist's chair and that gives the hero time to unshackle himself, or let his friends pop in through the window – and right triumphs. Real life isn't like that, is it?'

'No,' said Harry, 'although it must have been satisfying for Achmet Pasha to unburden himself. Those words are the sort of thing you might have wished you'd said, but he had no time for *l'esprit d'escalier* . . .'

'Right, ladies and gentlemen,' said Eric, hurrying behind the bar. 'What are you having?'

'Do you like it here?' asked Jessica.

'Do I?' said Eric, glancing over his shoulder as he pressed up the brandy optic. 'Yes, it's very peaceful after Telford. I used to be in engineering, then I got on the sales side and it all got me down.' He was glad to be able to state his case aloud. It went some way to making him believe it.

'Don't you ever feel lonely?' asked Jessica.

'Lonely?' said Eric stoutly. 'Not I. No time.'

'No, I suppose not,' said Jessica.

'No problem,' said Eric.

'Will you have one yourself?' invited Harry.

'I believe I will,' said Eric, as though drinking alcoholic liquor was foreign to his nature, 'and no cold tea for me today. I'll have a brandy, and here's to your healths.'

'Cheers,' said Jessica, lugubriously. She lit one of her cigarettes and when she'd smoked that she had another, which made her feel slightly ill. 'I'm going for a walk,' she said.

'I must go and tidy away some papers,' said Harry. 'I'll see you at lunch.'

★

Jessica walked in the green Christmas morning with her coat unbuttoned and her spirits round her ankles. 'Cursed, cowardly dogs . . .' she said under her breath, 'I fear you not.' She walked and walked, but the oppression went with her. She came to one of the rock formations for which the island was admired: it started at ground level and rose gradually, and then abruptly, until it terminated in a sheer drop to the snarling waves, foaming round its feet. Jessica walked, then climbed until she had reached its limit, where she sat down, out of breath, and lit another cigarette in the soggy stillness. She was coughing so hard that she could hear nothing. The turf was damp, the view unimpressive. She wouldn't have cared if she died.

Jon lay on his stomach in a small, wet declivity where the rock just started to rise. From here he could not see Jessica, but he knew where she was. He had followed her, had stood and watched her until she reached the heights and had stopped.

He was, he told himself, displeased with Jessica. She was not, he reminded himself, a particularly good actress, and she had no grace: she was, he considered, in all probability a lesbian. He had for a while intended to remonstrate with her and demand to know why she pretended not to desire him; to confront her and insist that she gave up all subterfuge, but now that he saw her sitting on the edge of a cliff he thought the best thing he could do would be to push her off. The move would undoubtedly teach her a lesson. He began to crawl forward.

Jessica finished her cigarette and threw the butt down into the sea, watching it as it fell. The sizzle as ember met water would be inaudible from where she sat, but she could imagine it. 'I curse you,' she remarked aloud, experimentally, 'and the foul harlots that bore you . . .'

Jon, hearing her talking to herself, concluded that she was crazy as well as devious, and was reaching out a hand when he felt he was being watched. There was a seal out there with an unblinking eye on him. He hesitated . . .

'What on earth possessed you to climb so high?' inquired Harry, panting a little. His daily walks in Hyde Park kept him fit, but he was no longer a young man.

'Crikey,' said Jessica, turning and noting that she now had two companions. 'Piccadilly Circus.' She looked at Jon and then looked away, embarrassed.

'I nearly didn't make it,' said Harry. 'I'd forgotten how the rock rises.'

'I thought you were fiddling with your papers,' said Jessica.

'Got bored,' said Harry, getting his breath back.

Jon smiled straight at him. 'It's nice up here,' he said, 'isn't it?'

'Yes,' said Harry.

'We can walk home together,' said Jessica. 'I hope all this exercise has given you an appetite for lunch.'

They caught up with Ronald and Anita on the way back to the inn. Anita was waving her hands around and speaking shrilly. '. . . I tell you that's where the cottage was,' she was saying. 'I remember the wall ending there and the tree on one side and the pillar box on the other . . .'

'It isn't there now,' said Ronald, obviously not for the first time.

'I *know* it isn't there now,' said Anita, 'but it *was*. I saw it. I spoke to the woman. She was knitting a sweater for her man and she spoke to me. She was eating a cough sweet – I smelt it. She gave me a cup of tea.'

'It must have been further along the road,' said Ronald.

'There isn't any further along the road . . .' said Anita, but she stopped arguing as the others came level.

'Nice walk?' asked Jessica.

'Yes, thank you,' said Anita. 'Most refreshing.'

'How far did you go?' asked Jessica, noting that these two fellow travellers had clearly been having a row, and adopting a friendly, eirenic tone.

135

'Right to where the little road stops,' said Anita.

'Not as far as the castle ruins, then,' said Jessica.

'No,' said Anita.

'Oh,' said Jessica. She stumbled and Harry took her elbow to steady her. 'These shoes aren't as sensible as they look,' she said. 'It's a funny sort of Christmas day,' she continued as no one else said anything. 'I keep thinking there ought to be children. I haven't seen any since I came.'

They passed a field with some cows in it and she wondered if Harry had once taken his little boy on the Eve of Christmas to see them kneeling in the stable, except that cows didn't frequent stables much these days and she hadn't noticed a stable in the Manse yard. Perhaps they knelt in the fields. When they lay down it meant it was going to rain. It was raining; a thin drizzle was drifting down from the hills.

'Oh hell,' said Jessica, buttoning her coat, 'why are those lying cows standing up? They're supposed to lie down when it's going to rain.'

'I expect they stand up when it starts,' said Anita, her temper improving as they neared the inn.

The regulars were in the bar. Ronald was saddened to see that his would-be analysand was among them. She became animated when she saw him. 'When are you going to tell my fortune then?' she cried.

'He's not a soothsayer,' said Anita, wondering why the girl did not turn her attentions to the golden-haired Jon if she wasn't getting any change out of the professor. Although she had fallen a little in love with Ronald, she couldn't see that he might have any attractions for anyone else. The girl looked her up and down and again dismissed her as negligible. She didn't much care for Jessica either: she had recognized her but was damned if she'd give her any satisfaction by saying so, not being what could be called a woman's woman. Anita, who had grown accustomed to thinking of herself in spinsterish terms — although she would not have put it like that —

imagined that more red-blooded females, well, the tarty sort, would have found Jon irresistible, and here she did herself less than justice: most females, when they had got over the shock of his beauty, found Jon unsatisfactory. Ronald, who if not much fun was undeniably masculine, approximated more closely to what they thought they were looking for.

'Why are you so quiet?' asked Jessica of Harry.

'I was thinking,' said Harry. 'I was thinking you'd be wise not to find yourself alone with that boy. Come and sit down.'

'I know,' said Jessica, following him to a table. 'I told you . . .'

'I don't mean that,' said Harry. 'He followed you today. I went straight upstairs after you'd gone, looked out of the window and he was following you. Now that would've been all right, nothing wrong in that, you might say, just looking for a little companionship on a walk – only he wasn't trying to catch up with you. I found it worrying.'

'I see,' said Jessica. She could – she could see Jon in dark sweater and pants, following her, out of earshot, careful to keep out of sight in case she should turn. He would have been in the role of a secret agent, a guerrilla, a member of the SAS or possibly a Red Indian brave. She remembered the look on his face when eventually she had turned to find him behind her, and Harry speaking. She had seen that look before – once when she had refused to climb with him to the top where the snow lay, and once . . .

'What is it?' asked Harry, as she was quiet.

'I remember where I met him before,' she said. 'It was a party after some commercial. I was drunk – we were all drunk. He must've been playing some part in the thing – I don't remember what, and I was talking to him in a corner when Mike – he's my boyfriend – came and said it was time to go home. He – Jon – had that look on his face then. I must have said goodbye, I'll ring you, or something, and we left. I do that sometimes. I tell people I'll ring them and I don't and they resent it. It was all quite trivial.'

'I thought he might have been going to push you over,' said Harry.

'Crikey,' said Jessica.

'Although I could of course be wrong,' said Harry.

'And there was me worrying because the other two had had a little tiff,' said Jessica. 'How ironical.' She felt not afraid, but annoyed. 'He's got a cheek,' she said. 'If anyone was going to murder me I'd prefer it to be somebody I knew well, somebody with some *real* cause.' She imagined herself hurtling into the sea, propelled by the hand of a bit-part actor. 'And they'd never have known,' she said. 'They'd have thought it was an accident – all my own fault for wearing silly shoes.'

'So keep away from him,' said Harry.

'What can I do about it?' asked Jessica.

'Just keep away,' said Harry. 'He can be accused of nothing but walking in a stealthy fashion.'

'And wearing a funny look on his face,' said Jessica. 'It's like those cases you read about where the police say they can't take any action until the person has killed you. I see now why the intended victims get so wrought up about it. They usually have much more than me to complain about, and I feel really cross only because he *may* have had the impertinence to try and murder me. How shall I comport myself towards him?'

'It's unprecedented in my experience,' said Harry. 'I've met the enemy after the war and we've had a drink together, but there was nothing personal in the hostilities.'

'It feels almost as bad as being raped,' said Jessica. 'A gross intrusion on one's privacy. Where is he now?'

'Seems to have disappeared again,' said Harry, looking round. 'He's nowhere to be seen.'

'It's rather sinister the way he disappears,' said Jessica, scoring another black mark against him. 'I'm going to buy you a pint for saving my life. I didn't think I much cared

138

about it earlier in all this damp, but now I feel I would've missed it badly.'

'You're young,' said Harry, 'with your life before you.'

'Oh, come on,' said Jessica. 'You're at it again. I must be nearly half-way through, only now I find I want to sit through the second half – see what happens – for instance, what's for lunch?'

'Turkey,' suggested Harry.

'I think Eric'll be more subtle than that,' said Jessica. 'You forget we're not doing Christmas.'

'Melon,' said Eric, 'consommé, roast beef, potatoes and carrots and peas, trifle, cheese and biscuits, coffee, and I don't give a damn.'

He had originally intended to serve thin slices of marinated salmon, a hot and herby soup, a haunch of venison from the supermarket on the mainland and bread-and-butter pudding with brandy in it, but he couldn't be bothered: he had discovered for himself what most women know – that to cook well and with imagination you have to be in a cheerful and contented frame of mind, and thus inclined to be generous. Things were getting Eric down to the point where he was beginning to think in terms of oven chips and frozen cod in batter and Walls ice-cream. Why not? he asked himself as despair crept up like an unwholesome tide. The longer Mabel was away the more he remembered her as really rather sweet: her ferocious aspects dimmed by her absence and his own loneliness. Finlay's sister-in-law, to whom he had addressed this reminder of the menu, had restored the Raeburn to life and was cutting up two melons, discarding the bruised parts.

Eric morosely fondled the beef to ensure that it had thawed properly and wondered about Christmas day in Glasgow. He was glad of the assistance offered by Finlay and his sister-in-law, without which he would have been lost, but he could not rid himself of an ungracious sense of faint resentment: it

139

seemed to him that the pair of them behaved as though they owned the place, not in any flamboyantly possessive style, but with a quietly secure assumption of right of tenure. They knew where everything was, and went about their business without ever referring to him, silently assured except when Finlay drank too much and gave vent to utterances which, while largely meaningless to Eric, were treated by his sister-in-law as indiscreet. This in turn made Eric feel rather like the victim of a conspiracy, as though something was going on under his nose about which he knew nothing. The island mentality, he thought, fearing that he was developing paranoid tendencies and wondering whether he should refer them to Ronald. Did he have any horseradish sauce or had they used it all up with yesterday's smoked mackerel? He didn't give a monkey's.

He left Finlay's sister-in-law opening tins of consommé to which he would later add, in order to take the taste away, a good slurp of sherry, and went reluctantly to the bar. You'd think that the owner of an inn, particularly one at the edge of the world, might feel like the captain of a ship in sole charge of the crew and passengers, but he didn't: he felt like a small, sad and put-upon person, reeking of kitchen steam and harassed almost to death. His expectations were disappointed – not of his guests, for on the whole they were more than he could have hoped for – but of his own response, since he had had a confident image of himself in the mode of those urbane and self-confident owner/chefs of pastel-painted restaurants, mingling on equal terms with the customers and gracefully (although always with wit) accepting their sycophantic observations. There were, as there always had been, chefs of uncertain temper who threw the hollandaise about when the fish had not arrived on time or a punter demanded the salt, but Eric had not aspired to such self-indulgence. He'd just wanted a peaceful, profitable and possibly satisfying time. Fantasy was self-defeating. That morning the strange boy had passed again on the way to the sea and Eric wished he'd gone fishing with him.

Nevertheless the scene in the bar was less dispiriting than his imaginings in the kitchen. The people, whether due to an excess of liquor the night before or because of some residual awareness of the nature of the season, were being well-behaved and polite to each other. Even the professor and Mrs H. were conversing in low, equable tones, while a girl had pinned Ronald into a corner and was addressing him earnestly. Jessica was looking rosily bright and positive and more like an actress than usual, while Anita was questioning Jon about some aspect of the island's topography. Harry, as always, was his gentlemanly self, unfailingly polite and reassuringly sane.

'You had it back at the end of August, you creep,' Mrs H. was saying. 'Finlay took it down on the back of the tractor.'

'No, he didn't,' said the professor. 'I was looking for it this morning and it's not there.'

'Well, I haven't got it,' said Mrs H. 'You must've left it somewhere.'

'How could I leave it somewhere?' said the professor. 'It's not the sort of thing you leave somewhere.'

'How do I know?' said Mrs H. 'How do I know what you do with things you borrow?'

'*You* borrowed it from *me*,' said the professor. 'I bought it from you last year and then you borrowed it back.'

'Then I gave it back,' said Mrs H. 'Finlay took it down on . . .'

'He didn't,' said the professor. 'I'd've remembered.'

This was not an unusual discussion on the island where people were constantly borrowing things from each other – items of machinery to move boats around, mow grass, mend the guttering, replace the aerials. It was perhaps a primitive form of social intercourse.

'I expect it'll turn up,' said Mrs H. 'Whose round is it?'

'Yours,' said the professor.

Ronald was asking himself yet again why people should imagine he might be interested in their dreams. He wasn't even interested in his own dreams. He was interested in lunch and frequently consulted his watch without bothering to be surreptitious.

'. . . so then I flew to the top of the chimney,' said the girl. 'I expect that's very significant.' She awaited his diagnosis, gazing at him.

'What do you make the time?' asked Ronald.

'What would that prove?' asked the girl. '*I* make it 12.30. What does that tell you?'

Ronald gazed back at her, bewildered, while she awaited his pronouncement.

'That it's 12.30,' he said. His watch said the same.

She pondered on the profundity of this as she drank her rum and Coke: she had heard somewhere that psychiatrists seldom said much to their patients, marshalling the salient psychological facts in neat order and leaving it to them to realize the significance for themselves; to recall the forgotten events which re-emerged in dreams in disguised form. Something must once have happened to her at 12.30, something to do with a chimney . . .

'I can't imagine how I should be feeling,' said Jessica. 'I don't think anyone ever tried to murder me before. They may have wanted to, if we're being perfectly honest, but they never tried it on. If I was *acting* someone who someone had just tried to murder I'd know how to behave, but as it is I only feel a bit insulted. It doesn't seem normal somehow. Shouldn't I be clutching my throat and moaning with terror?'

'Not now,' said Harry. 'Everyone would be very surprised unless you went on to explain.'

'It would positively *ruin* Christmas lunch, would it not?' said Jessica.

'It would certainly go some way towards putting a damper on the proceedings,' agreed Harry. 'You must just be careful to stay away from him. I don't suppose he'll try it again.' In saying this Harry was assuming that Jon, apart from the occasional aberration, was basically as sane as himself.

Jessica was for once more clear-sighted. 'Not if he's nuts,' she said. 'If he's nuts he'll go on doing it. Maybe he's got an *idée fixe* and nothing will do but that he should murder his mother.'

'You're not his mother,' Harry pointed out.

'He may *think* I am,' said Jessica. 'He may identify me with his mother who locked him in the coal cellar when he was an infant child so that she could have a cocktail in peace with a gentleman caller – or possibly she had another little tot whom she liked better and she took it to the pictures while he . . .' she found she didn't want to say his name '. . . cried in the coal dust until his face got positively filthy, and then when she came back she smacked him for getting dirty. I probably resemble her. What's he doing now?'

Harry looked across the room to where Jon leaned against the bar. 'He's talking to Anita,' he said. In this he was less than accurate. Anita was doing most of the talking.

'You go on down the road until you come to the part where the sign's fallen down. If you bend over to look at it it says something about the castle, but because it's fallen down you can't tell which way it's pointing, so you go on up a little road until it stops, and there's a cottage there . . .'

'Is there?' said Jon, sucking a swizzle-stick absent-mindedly, and thinking of broken bones.

'If you've been up there you must have seen it,' said Anita. 'You couldn't miss it. Did you see it?'

'I honestly can't remember,' said Jon. He never liked to give the impression that there was something he didn't know, even if it was only the whereabouts of a tumbledown cottage on the way to a fallen castle. 'I must've passed it but I was thinking about something else.'

'It's so exasperating,' said Anita. 'I *might* have gone another way and got mixed up, but I can't believe it. I really wanted to look at those sweaters again. They knit them in different patterns so when their man gets washed up they can . . .'

'So you said,' said Jon.

'Do you suppose,' whispered Jessica to Harry, 'that, with any luck, he might transfer his feelings of filial murderousness to Anita? No, forget I said that,' she added. 'That wasn't very nice. I didn't mean it – not really, not altogether.'

'He shows no signs at the moment,' said Harry. 'He's going out again.'

'I wonder where he goes,' said Jessica. 'Maybe he goes looking for mothers to murder. I don't think there are many round here since there aren't any children.'

'A lot of the young people leave,' said Harry. 'It's hard for them to make a living now. A bit of farming, a bit of fishing . . .'

'How does Finlay manage?' asked Jessica, as he came into the bar in his antique oilskins.

'He does a bit of everything,' said Harry. 'Anything that needs to be done – if Finlay's sober, he'll do it.'

'It must give him a lovely sense of power,' said Jessica. 'What sort of thing?' she added as she found she was unrealistically visualizing Finlay as a creature of myth, ensuring that the corn sprang at the expected time, the blossom bloomed correctly and finally transformed itself into fruit, and the tides turned when Finlay bade the moon to cause them to do so.

'More or less anything,' said Harry. 'There are people like that in most small communities. There have to be or no one would survive. And then there's his sister-in-law – she copes with confinements and medical emergencies when the doctor can't get across.'

'Like the blacksmith and the wise woman,' said Jessica, back in the ravelled realms of ancient legend.

'Very like,' said Harry, finishing his beer.

Finlay had removed his outer covering and was leaning on the bar: he was wearing a shapeless knitted garment with a few stray fish-scales adhering to the wool. Anita peered at it as closely as was compatible with the usages of polite society and inquired whether his woman had knitted it for him. Finlay, who was sober as yet, replied, as far as Anita could tell, that, on the contrary, she had bought it for him from the Oxfam shop in the town. Anita was quite sure he was lying.

'What'll you have, Finlay?' asked Eric, hoping he wasn't planning to get drunk, since he had chopped up a great deal of driftwood for the fires that morning and sometimes seemed to assume that this task gave him licence to drink whisky for the rest of the day.

'Whusky,' said Finlay as Eric had foretold.

'I think I may have a whisky too, please,' said Ronald, sidling away from the girl who was presently trying to recall a pre-birth experience.

'You shouldn't drink whisky before lunch,' said Anita. 'Put a lot of ice in it,' she instructed Eric, wondering whether she could maintain her newfound authoritativeness when she returned to her department, if indeed, she ever did decide to return. She felt a new Anita emerging from the sloughed persona of the old, as bossing Ronald about gradually increased her confidence and self-esteem. Ronald briefly clasped her hand.

Gazing into the depths of her steaming tinned consommé Jessica pondered on her emotional condition. Being murdered, or rather suspecting that somebody was harbouring murderous thoughts towards you, was, she concluded, *extraordinarily* depressing. Jon was seated on the opposite side of the table in front of the window with the ladder fern behind him and she gave him an old-fashioned look. He stared back without blinking and Jessica looked away. Perhaps she should go into hiding; change her name and her appearance, buy some new clothes and settle in a small mining town somewhere in the north. She could get a job in a corner shop and gradually work her way up, marry the owner and sit on a high stool behind the counter wearing a black satin dress and growing stout. She realized that she had thoughtlessly superimposed a Gallic image on the fugitive that she was to become and adjusted her mental processes. It would have to be a Crimplene dress and a cardigan. On the other hand she could always flee to Provence and marry a shopkeeper there: but what if he was married already? Then, by some strange coincidence Jon would be hitch-hiking through the French countryside, or taking part in a commercial for something instant, in a package, with a Provençal flavour, indulging, in his spare time, his penchant for murdering mothers, and he would push, not her, but the shopkeeper's wife out of an olive tree . . .

Eric moved round, pouring sherry: it tasted very similar to the soup, which wasn't surprising because he had absent-mindedly poured more of it than he had intended into the consommé as it simmered. Nobody seemed to mind: their thoughts, mostly, were elsewhere.

'This is very good,' said Ronald.

Anita smiled at him indulgently. His wife must have been a bad housekeeper if he meant it sincerely. She could show him what was really good – proper soup made from a ham-bone, cooked slowly and skimmed carefully; fresh salads and bean stew and *coq au vin* and all sorts of things that took hours to prepare with tenderness and skill. When they were married she would never be cross with him, never let him see if he irritated her, never say a harsh word to him. They could be very happy together once she had cured him of a few faults: she would do that before the wedding and then they could get on with life without distraction. As the wife of a psychoanalyst she would have no need to work, either for financial reasons or to give herself something to think about.

She might make him shave off his beard because he had soup in it, and in the evenings they would discuss the theories of Freud.

Harry was thinking of Christmasses past with the resignation of the *mutilé de guerre* whose life, previous to the catastrophe, had given no cause for complaint. He had never triumphed in his loss as some people do, saying, 'There, I told you so. Everything has always been against me, and now *this*.' He had accepted the deaths with a sense of surprise that anything could hurt so much and had gone on living, albeit with some reluctance. He praised God for bringing death to all the children of men, for if only some were taken the rest would live lives of raging madness, tortured by loss and burning with horror at the strange thing . . .

'What are you thinking about?' asked Jon, and everyone looked at him, wondering to whom he had spoken. 'You,' he said, staring at Harry.

'I believe I was thinking about Christmas,' said Harry. 'Only we are forbidden to mention the subject, are we not?'

'I'm getting tired of not mentioning it,' said Jessica. 'It feels like a funeral with everyone trying not to mention the body or its name, or even if it ever existed alive, or why they're there. I feel that if I said "Happy Christmas" it would be unladylike.'

'You weren't thinking about that,' said Jon, but he said it softly, to himself and not to Harry, and no one took any notice of him because they were suddenly all speaking at once.

'We always had turkey,' Ronald was saying, 'with stuffing and some sort of jam. It took my wife hours of preparation the night before.' He spoke with melancholy pride, as though of Florence Nightingale and the conditions at Scutari.

'It really isn't very difficult,' Anita told him sharply. 'Not if you organize it properly. I always have the menu clear in my head from the beginning of November.'

'We didn't have Christmas pudding because she didn't like it,' said Ronald regretfully. 'We used to have some sort of cake with nuts in it.'

'If you want Christmas pudding I can organize that,' said Eric, bearing in the plates of roast beef. He had two left over from last year: Christmas pudding never went off, and even if it had, he thought, he would have no hesitation in offering it to this perverse, ungrateful, irrational mob. He hoped they might choke.

'I hate Christmas pudding,' said Jessica. 'And I don't want nuts and crackers and wishbones. I just feel odd pretending nothing's happening out of the ordinary.'

Eric relented a little, towards her at least: she was making some attempt to play the game according to the rules they had tacitly agreed.

'They never celebrate Christmas here,' he told them again. 'They never have.'

'Why?' asked Anita, and Eric confessed that he didn't really know. 'Does anyone know?' she said.

'It's partly a hang-over from fundamental Protestantism,' said Harry. 'There was a time when everyone round here worked on Christmas day, but that was when everyone worked on all the other days as well . . .'

'And partly what else?' asked Anita as he stopped speaking.

'Partly a relic of paganism,' said Harry. 'The old beliefs never really died out until the ferry made the place accessible to strangers.'

'What old beliefs?' asked Anita.

'You'll have to ask Finlay,' said Harry.

'I can't understand anything Finlay says,' said Anita. 'And I don't think he'd tell me anyway.'

Harry knew that.

'It's the island mentality,' said Eric, bringing in the vegetables. 'They all hang together,' and the others knew what he meant by this seeming irrelevance for they, too, had felt the sense of exclusion which troubled him. Only Harry appeared momentarily set apart as they sensed he knew too much and too little, and would tell them nothing; would not share either his awareness or his doubt. He had been here before, had left and returned, and dimly they wondered whether he was flesh or fowl or good red herring: one of them, or aligned with the islanders. Harry also wondered, but he had felt like something of a stranger on the face of the earth for a long time now: he was used to it.

'The collective unconscious,' began Ronald, who was nothing if not eclectic, 'may in some circumstances, congenial to the de-suppression of the individual unconscious, surface without the realization of the participants, and without trauma to what could be termed the psychic tissue of the community, and express itself in group activity.' He meant by this to evoke an image of those tribal manifestations of an ancient culture, whose roots are obscured in the past; where the living members of the tribe, having led secluded lives, carry on in much the same way as their ancestors did in the year dot; painting themselves, doing war-dances, placating their deities and behaving in what seems to themselves, if to no one else, an entirely reasonable fashion. To Jessica, however, his final words had conjured up a vision of the charismatic movement in the church, of bearded people falling trustfully backwards into other people's arms in encounter sessions, of Americans saying earnestly, 'We must *talk*,' and similar distressing scenes. She shuddered.

'Are you cold?' inquired Anita: she had considered Ronald's contribution both scholarly and enlightening, although she hadn't understood it.

'Goose over my grave,' explained Jessica, wishing she could stop thinking about death and still blaming Jon, basically, for her lowness of spirit. 'It's just clannishness,' she said. 'Peasants are always clannish. If you stay in any village you'll feel like an outsider.'

'I don't find that,' said Anita. 'I find most people are willing to accept you if you're open and friendly towards them.' She knew that this was not so, but she thought it should be: she also wished to indicate to Ronald that she was good with people because this could only be a useful quality in the wife of a psychoanalyst.

'There's a storm brewing,' said Eric as he came to carry away the vegetable dishes. 'It's getting dark outside. We may be in for some snow.'

It was too late now for the full glamour of snow, but even a little might stay in their memories, leave them with a picture of the inn roof innocently white rather than rope grey, the whole island lost in a christening gown instead of the threadbare subfusc of dead grass and naked branches. When he had first seen it it had been clad in leaves and now, sometimes, when he thought of it he saw, not the reality, but the green slopes under a sky as bright as silk. It was the same with his wife: often now he thought of her as she had been when they first met and not of the pale, discontented creature she had become. Eric occasionally wished he had less imagination: it would make everyday life less painful.

Finlay's sister-in-law removed the rest of the dishes and a hush fell over the table as those diners who could see through the window without undue contortion looked out at the darkening afternoon and listened to the rising wind. It occurred to them that, if conditions got really bad, they would not be able to leave for some days.

'Well . . .' said Harry. It mattered little to him if he couldn't get away, but he felt concern for the others: if they were forced to overstay they would lose whatever holiday feeling they had and begin to feel imprisoned. Years ago he had watched frustrated holidaymakers standing on the quay willing the ferry to brave the tossing waters and save them from exile, glum with the impotence of the castaway; luggage packed, bills paid, all ordered for departure and left in limbo with even the time they had enjoyed becoming devalued as it began to stretch meaninglessly on with no end in sight. He knew the feeling but, to him, it didn't matter where he was.

'If it does snow,' said Jon, 'perhaps I'll get in some skiing.'

'We've only got a day left,' said Anita.

'A day would do,' said Jon. He would cut a heroic figure swooping down the gleaming slopes on the last day. 'It's some time since I got to Klosters.'

'When did you last get to Klosters?' asked Ronald out of professional habit, before he could think what he was doing. The others again began to talk at once.

'If it only snows,' said Anita, 'that won't stop us going, will it?'

'Listen to the wind,' said Jessica.

'I go most years,' said Jon, and the rest of them who, being human, were all accustomed to lying with a greater or lesser degree of skill, wondered, not why he did it, but why he did it so badly. Anita in particular hoped uneasily that she was not as transparent when she veered from the truth, while Jessica thought that if he hadn't tried to murder her she would possibly have taught him better, both from the kindness of her heart and out of respect for the business of acting. Ronald, whose task in life was the dissection of other people's fantasies and the overt acceptance of what is known as reality, applied himself to his pudding, wondering whether dentists, when off duty, felt inclined to advise comparative strangers about the unwisdom of sucking sweets. Habit was harder to break than he had realized.

Jessica, seeing Jon framed by the ladder fern, perceived him for a moment as a cross between a damned nuisance and a jungle beast: someone who wished to kill you was worse than, although not dissimilar to, the hotel bore; necessitating caution and a wearying degree of circumspection as you endeavoured to keep out of his way, creeping round corners on stockinged feet and squinting into rooms before you dared enter for fear that he would pounce. It was such *cheek*, thought Jessica; such an intrusion on privacy. And as for jungle beasts – she had no objection to them as long as they stayed in the undergrowth, gnawing the decaying carcases of wildebeest, but once they developed a taste for human flesh they could not be ignored. She found that she was beginning to hate him and fought against it, not wishing to allow such intimacy between them. She looked at him but his eyes were blank, his thoughts elsewhere. He was probably engaged in leaping a snow-clad precipice with a box of poisoned chocolates clutched between his teeth, on his way to present them to an older woman. Jessica wasn't far wrong.

'I think we should drink to our host,' said Harry as the pudding plates were removed.

Eric stood smiling modestly, rather wishing he had given them a better lunch, but thankful that they hadn't seemed to notice its shortcomings. 'As long as you're enjoying your-selves . . .' he said.

Jessica retired to her room with *The Tenant of Wildfell Hall* and the taste of port in her mouth. Huntingdon's excesses, she noted, had finally caught up with him and he was – most reluctantly – about to die: apart from a natural disinclination to do this he was gripped by a terror of Hell and kept imploring his wife to save him. Every now and then he told himself that the after-life was all a fable, but doubt assailed him. Poor man, thought Jessica, but he was so demanding and unreasonable that she began to feel sympathy for Helen who despite her sanctimoniousness was clearly a good sort. If anyone had addressed Jessica as his 'immaculate angel' and gone on to remark, '. . . when once you have secured your reward, and find yourself safe in heaven, and me howling in hell-fire, catch you lifting a finger to serve me then . . .' she would have left him to rot, but Helen kept the door ajar, snatching an hour or so of sleep whenever she could, and never once snapped back. Jessica read on, growing more depressed, until Huntingdon had met his end, '. . . none can imagine the miseries, both bodily and mental, of the deathbed! How could I endure to think that that poor trembling soul was hurried away to everlasting torment? It would drive me mad!'

'Harry,' said Jessica, at the door of his room, 'could I have a B and S?' She made no apology.

'You don't look well,' observed Harry.

'I'm all right,' she said. 'Only I've just been reading about Hell again. I think nineteenth-century Hell is probably worse than the Hell of other ages – like nineteenth-century medicine – just beginning to be modern so they tried every which way to keep you alive and you couldn't die as fast as you'd have liked. They were always experimenting with new methods to prolong the agony. How do I know that? Is it true, do you suppose? What's it got to do with Hell anyway?'

'I don't know,' said Harry, 'but I see what you mean.'

'Diphtheria and whooping cough and scarlet fever and caustics and disinfectant, and all the curtains drawn, and the fear of Hell,' said Jessica. 'I know what today feels like. It feels like a Protestant's Sunday. No joy. Worse – a reminder of Hell. I shan't try and skip Christmas again, it isn't worth it.'

'Gordon was good on hell,' said Harry. 'Shall I tell you?'

'Will it cheer me up?' asked Jessica.

'It might,' said Harry.

'I'm not sure if I'm frightened of death or Hell,' said Jessica, 'or both, or neither, or whether I've merely got indigestion, or maybe I was last incarnated in some Victorian villa with bad drains, and I can't shake the memory off. Tell me about Gordon and Hell.'

Harry turned to his notes. ' "I may say . . ." ' he read, ' ". . . I have died suddenly over a hundred times; but in these deaths I have never felt the least doubt of our salvation. Nothing can be more abject and miserable than the usual conception of God. Accept what I say – namely, that He has put us in a painful position (I believe with our perfect consent, for if Christ came to do His will, so did we, His members) to learn what He is, and that He will extricate us. Imagine to yourself, what pleasure would it be to Him to burn us or to torture us? Can we believe any *human being* capable of creating us for such a purpose? Would it show his power? Why, He is omnipotent! Would it show His justice? He is righteous – no one will deny it. We credit God with attributes which are utterly hateful to the meanest of men. Looking at our darkness of vision, how can He be what we credit Him with? I quite wonder at the long time it has taken us to see that the general doctrine of the Church is so erroneous." I suppose the climate of opinion at the time was still clouded by Calvinism.'

'I wonder if he believed in the transmigration of souls?' said Jessica, who had lived with a Buddhist convert for a while.

'I shouldn't be surprised,' said Harry.

'I wonder if the churchmen were mad with him?' said Jessica, entertaining an image of a crowd of the clergy wearing shovel-hats and clutching hymn books, pursuing a camel-mounted Gordon through a wilderness of dust.

'If they were they probably couldn't say much,' said Harry, 'because during and after Khartoum he was the darling of the public.'

'I wonder if I'll ever be the darling of the public,' said Jessica, selfishly, 'or would that only mean that more people would want to murder me?'

And Harry, much as he liked her, wished that she would go away and read her book, for he had his own thoughts to contend with.

It was getting beyond a joke. Jon had stood for nearly an hour in his room with the door ajar, watching and waiting for Jessica to emerge from Harry's room. He was conscious of no discomfort, but stood quite still behind the door, unblinking, and looking madder than usual, as people are wont to do when they stand too long without moving, their heads poked forward and their gaze glued to some expected or imaginary happening.

When at last Jessica appeared he still did not move but his eyes followed her as far as they could. She had passed beyond his vision when he heard her swear, and then she turned and came back. What she had done was to drift along the corridor with her hand on the banister rail and the key dangling from her finger, so not surprisingly she had dropped it into the hall. She walked back more swiftly, cursing. To Jon she bore the appearance of a person who has wrenched herself unwillingly from the beloved object, got to the end of the corridor, said to herself, 'Stuff it – *I won't* leave him,' and is on her way back to the aforesaid beloved object. He suddenly shut the door and turned to face the window, shaking with what might have seemed to an impartial observer like the onset of a fit. An observer would undoubtedly have considered his demeanour most alarming. Jessica found her key on the mat in the hall and walked back to her room, unseen by anyone. Jon, also unseen, permitted himself overt expression of his *malaise*: he grimaced and thrust at the air with his head and hands, and growled quietly. After a while he washed his face in cold water in the peat-stained basin, looking in the glass as he dried it. Now that he had an observer, even though it was only himself, he composed his features and watched them until they seemed normal again. After a while he went to Harry's room and stood with his ear to the door, listening for sounds of sinful rapture. There was no noise at all, so Jon found the silence even more suggestive than sound would have been, opened the door without knocking and went in. Harry was standing looking out of the window, but to Jon the room had an unfinished air since there was no sign of Jessica with her clothes off and her hair tumbled. He had been so certain that she would be there, had had such a clear vision of *how* she would be that he thought her absence a hallucination, and stepped forward with his hands outstretched, feeling for her invisible presence.

'Yes?' said Harry.

'Where is she?' said Jon, turning round and turning again.

'She isn't here,' said Harry.

'She is . . .' said Jon, and stopped with the caution of the madman. He said reasonably, 'You're much too old for her, you know.'

Harry watched him and said nothing.

'Not that she's so young,' continued Jon, 'but you're too old for her.' He lowered his voice. 'She's a nymphomaniac, isn't she?' he said. 'She comes to my room in the night . . .' he stopped again, not sure that that was what he had meant to say. 'You've got a good view from here,' he observed, joining Harry by the window. 'You can watch them coming from the shore.' He hadn't meant to say that either and closed his eyes for a second. 'I've been drinking,' he confided after a while as Harry still said nothing. 'I've been drinking a bottle of whisky and eating peanuts. She'll be angry when she sees how much I've drunk and I haven't left any peanuts for her. She'll say . . .' He laid his hand against the cold of the window pane. 'There's someone watching me out there,' he said. 'Out in the sea. They have grey eyes – grey as the sea. They're looking at me.'

'The owl was a baker's daughter,' said Harry.

'Yes, she was,' said Jon, unsurprised at this disclosure. Then he left.

Harry stayed by the window, looking out to sea – to where the grey eyes were watching. He wondered what he should do.

It was night-time in the bar and outside the snow was at last beginning to fall, bringing an illusion of warmth and safety to the denizens of the inn.

'Isn't this cosy,' said Mrs H., taking off her anorak to reveal a blue dress, sequinned on the shoulders and hips. It was, supposed Jessica, what is known as a cocktail frock, one of a species now largely extinct except on remote islands. 'I'd've thought they'd shot the last one years ago,' she said to herself, feeling out of place again; lost and defenceless in the alien and unfashionable ambience. 'It must have been hiding in a corner all lonely and afraid. It's probably terrified now that a collector will bag it . . .'

'Did you have a nice lunch?' asked Mrs H. 'I've left John washing up.' She looked round to see if by any chance there were any new men available for the evening and was disappointed, though unastonished. 'What a dump,' she said, not critically nor even sadly, but as one remarking on a fact. Eric frowned but did not contradict her.

'Sorry,' said Jessica, 'I was thinking about something else. What did you say?'

'I said, did you have a nice lunch,' repeated Mrs H.

'Very nice,' said Jessica. 'Did you?'

'It was all right,' said Mrs H. 'He overcooked the sprouts but I don't really mind that. I don't like vegetables the way they do them now – just show them the hot water and slap them in front of you.'

'*Al dente*,' said Eric, defensively.

'Undercooked,' said Mrs H. 'Doesn't even kill the germs.'

'Some vegetables are better raw,' said Anita, 'if you wash them well.'

'We have a murderer in our midst,' said Jessica.

'Pardon,' said Mrs H.

'I was thinking aloud,' said Jessica. 'It's a line from my new play.'

'Sounds interesting,' said Mrs H.

'Sometimes you only need to blanch them,' said Anita.

'My wife used to cook little marrows – in a lot of butter, I think,' said Ronald, reminiscently.

'Courgettes,' said Anita. 'I do them with garlic and tomatoes.' She hated Ronald's wife.

'I wonder if you can eat ladder fern,' said Jessica. They looked at her inquiringly. 'If you tied bits of it in bunches you could steam them like asparagus.'

'Why would you want to?' asked Anita.

'I don't really,' said Jessica, 'only there's such a lot of it about it seems a waste not to eat it.'

'You don't have to eat everything,' said Anita.

'I suppose not,' said Jessica. Only one more day and she could go home and see what Mike had been up to. She would stay close to Harry on the train and not go near the platform's edge in case Jon should take it upon himself to mince her under the train wheels. He had just come into the bar and was standing to one side, looking at her.

The professor entered with a girl in the duffel coat. He seemed annoyed and Jessica wondered what he had to be cross about when, so far as she knew, nobody was trying to kill him. At present she felt she was the only person in the world with something to be really cross about.

'They've been at it again,' he said. 'I nearly caught them this time. There's just enough snow to show up the footprints on the lawn.'

'They were playing music,' said the girl in the duffel coat unexpectedly.

'Bollocks,' said the professor. 'They weren't. It was the wind in the wires.' This was clearly the continuation of an argument which had begun earlier and was leading nowhere.

'They were,' said the girl, and Mrs H. brightened at the prospect of discord.

'It was probably the ghosts again,' she said. 'You're haunted.'

'I'm not haunted,' said the professor, as though he'd been accused of having lice. The distinction of having a ghost was obviously outweighed for him by the nuisance of trespass. If the dancers on his lawn came from another element he still resented them pushing his fence down. 'It's bloody-minded locals,' he said and stroked his crotch fretfully, which made Jessica think of Mike again. Perhaps it was the fault of the feminists, she thought, which caused so many men to have to keep publicly checking on their masculinity.

Mrs H. reached over and smacked his wrist. 'Don't do that,' she said in a playful voice.

'Bollocks,' said the professor.

Yes, thought Jessica, they did know each other well.

'What's happening?' asked Ronald becoming aware of tension.

'Someone keeps tearing down my fence,' said the professor. 'Some yobs.'

'If you didn't have a fence,' said Ronald, 'they couldn't tear it down.'

The professor didn't bother to answer him.

'To some personalities,' said Ronald, 'the mere fact of prohibition is sufficient to trigger an anti-social response. Without the challenge of imposed boundaries, what might be classed by the layman as the mentally subnormal – the "yobs" of whom you speak – will not even realize that an area is intended to lie beyond their reach and competence, and therefore their resentments do not become unmanageable.'

'He means that if you see a sign saying "Keep off the grass",' translated Anita who was beginning to understand his style after hours in his company, 'you won't. You'll walk on it because the sign says it's there. Isn't that so, Ronald?'

'That,' agreed Ronald, 'at its simplest, is more or less what I mean.'

'Bollocks,' insisted the professor, determined to retain his fence and embrace his grudge.

A chill draught swept into the bar and Jessica looked up to see who had come in. It was Finlay wearing his oilskins and lurching a little. He took his flute from a pocket and blew into it, whereupon his sister-in-law leaned across the counter and took it from him. He laughed, requesting whisky and she served him silently. 'Whaur's the colonel?' he said, looking about him. 'I hae a message.' His sister-in-law gave him a warning glance and he laughed again.

Eric watched them coldly. Their seemingly meaningless exchanges served, as always, to make him feel left out. He was overwhelmed by anticlimax and he wanted his wife even though she could be so disagreeable. He was lonely. 'I'm going to get some mineral water from the back,' he said, but nobody seemed to care.

It was snowing steadily in the inn yard and through the drifting flakes he could see the boy sitting on the wall. He watched him for a while and it seemed the boy watched him back, as the seals sometimes watched him when he stood on the foreshore, but neither of them spoke.

There was little conversation going on in the bar when he got back. Jon had said nothing all evening and the others seemed lost in private abstraction, except for Ronald and Anita, who were engrossed in some aspect of psychology, the one talking and the other wearing an intelligent expression. Jessica got to her feet suddenly. It had occurred to her that she had best make her escape to bed while there were people around to intervene if Jon's murderous impulses should be activated.

'Good night everyone,' she said and went quickly upstairs. She locked her door, tried it several times to make certain it was secure, then got into bed, but only to lie awake until dawn. She knew that Jon was close by and now she was cold with a bitter fear. Harry, too, stayed awake, his door a little open so that he would know should death be afoot.

Jessica got out of bed at first light and went to the window. The snow had come like a coquette, pale and pretty, and now had gone again. All joy and beauty, realized Jessica, went without excuse or explanation, leaving only drabness behind, as the retreating tide, whoring after the moon, left horrid and redundant things on the helpless sand. She had a really bad hangover due to her consumption of too much port.

'What's the matter?' asked Anita at breakfast. 'You look terrible.' Although her tone was compassionate it gave her quiet satisfaction to be able to say this, in perfect truth, to a fairly famous actress.

'I am terrible,' said Jessica, downing her glass of juice. It tasted, she thought, like the urine of demons.

'Would you like one of my vitamin pills?' asked Anita. 'They have everything.'

'Oh, all right,' said Jessica, holding out her palm. 'You mustn't let me drink anything today. If anyone sees me making for the bar he must stand in my way, shaking his head like this – *Ouch*.' She clutched her own head with both hands to steady it.

'Poor thing,' said Anita for Ronald's benefit: a quality of caring would be invaluable in the wife of a psychoanalyst.

'Alcohol is a depressant,' said Ronald.

'Life's a depressant,' said Jessica. She added, under her breath, 'Jessica's body was discovered this morning. She had shot herself after drinking too much lousy port and looked extremely beautiful and calm, considering the circumstances. With her death the theatre – or rather the world of commercial TV – has lost a luminous presence and nothing will ever be the same again. The other reason she shot herself is that a lunatic was trying to kill her and rather than submit to this gross impertinence she took the easy way out . . .'

'Did you say something?' asked Anita.

'Not really,' said Jessica.

'You were rehearsing lines again,' said Anita. 'You must be subconsciously worried about your play.'

'No, I'm not,' said Jessica. 'I was saying my morning prayers because I forgot earlier.' She had discovered when she was playing St Joan in rep that any mention of religious observance tended to silence people and make them uncomfortable.

'What are we going to do today?' asked Anita, turning to Ronald.

'I don't know,' said Ronald, polishing off the toast.

Jessica grew more depressed. It was obvious that Anita had decided to marry and had chosen Ronald. She knew the signs. Women who had determined to marry always behaved as Anita was behaving now – half proprietorial and half winsomely charming. She wondered if she ought to warn her: she could say, 'Don't do it. You won't like it, you know. It isn't any fun. You might think it's going to be now, but you'll soon learn better and by then it'll be too late. I *know*.' But anyone hell-bent on matrimony wouldn't believe her. In all probability Anita would think she wanted to marry Ronald herself, or at least prevent anyone else from being happy. Unexpectedly this reflection cheered Jessica. Things could be worse: she could have been married to Whiskers over there and have had to spend a lifetime watching him eat with his mouth open. But then Jon came in and her heart missed several beats in the way she supposed it was meant to when your life was threatened. He sat down by the ladder fern and wished everyone good morning in quite a sane fashion.

'So there'll be no skiing,' he said. 'The snow's all melted.'

'What a shame,' said Anita. She meant this sarcastically, but because she was so busy impressing Ronald with her sweetness of disposition she said it sympathetically. 'Perhaps you could think of something else exciting to do on your last day.' There, how was that for an expression of interest and concern in an undeserving person: she glanced at Ronald for approval but he was thinking about something else.

Thanks a lot, thought Jessica, he'd probably find it most exciting to make this my last day ever.

'I was just thinking,' said Ronald, seriously.

'What about?' asked Anita, laying down her napkin and

turning to him with the docile air of the potential bride intent on familiarizing herself with all the innermost workings of the mind of her mate-to-be.

'If we leave here at eleven tomorrow where will we have our lunch?' he said.

'We can have our lunch on the train,' said Anita tenderly, savouring the collective pronoun and taking it to include only herself and Ronald. She no longer felt confused by the way he changed from sage to greedy child for she was, she told herself, beginning truly to understand him and find all his ways endearing.

'I'll just have to get in some sailing,' said Jon, peering round the ladder fern at the dismal prospect of sea and cloud. 'I'll take Jessica for a spin round the headland.'

Oh no, you won't, thought Jessica, and she said aloud: 'I have to wash my hair.' Then she wished she'd thought of some other excuse, for she had a vision of Jon washing her hair eternally in all the foaming wastes of the Atlantic ocean. 'I want to finish reading my book before I leave,' she added. 'Here indoors where it's warm and dry.'

'You can watch me through the window,' said Jon, and he sounded not mad, but disconsolate and humble. Jessica felt a second of pity for the lost child before she pulled herself together.

'Schmuck,' said Ronald as Jon left the room, and Jessica was briefly diverted by this evidence of a different aspect to a character she thought she had summed up. He's human, she thought. Anita, however, found his remark lacking in dignity and professional finesse.

'He's unbalanced,' she reminded the psychoanalyst. 'He needs treatment.'

'He's a schmuck,' repeated Ronald stubbornly. Jon had reminded him of his least favourite patient, and by association, of the wifeless, cold and foodless house to which he must soon return. There was, he thought self-pityingly, nothing more depressed than a depressed psychoanalyst, for no one else was so familiar, by way of both observation and practice, with the subtle gradations and bleak possibilities of this melancholy state. He took the remains of a once-hot roll from Anita's plate and piled jam on it – an act which could be construed as displaying a heart-warming familiarity and ease of manner, or a lack of any knowledge of social decorum whatsoever. Anita couldn't make up her mind.

Jessica pushed aside the fronds of the ladder fern and looked out over the shore to where Finlay sat beside a broken rowing-boat, doing something of a probably nautical nature to a length of rope. On the other hand, mused Jessica, he might have been playing cat's cradle: he seemed, despite his reputation as man-of-all-work, to waste a shocking amount of time. He looked up towards the top windows of the inn and waved. Jessica heard Harry's tread on the stairs and watched as he went out of the front door to where Finlay sat, surrounded by the things of the sea. She wished she could hear what they were saying, Harry so grave, and Finlay throwing back his head and laughing at who knew what. As she stood there she began to feel something of the sense of exclusion of which Eric was always so conscious, and then as she stood longer she began to feel like a spy.

'What are you looking at?' asked Anita – so her espionage was apparent to others: she had stared too long and too intently.

'I was just watching the birds,' she said, looking upwards. 'They're all flying inland.' She turned towards the table and when she looked through the window again Finlay had gone and Harry stood alone, facing the sea as a rising wind lifted the hem of his coat.

She felt cold and wished she'd brought her cashmere sweater with her. When she'd packed it wouldn't go into her suitcase and she'd left it on the bed. She went to her room to get her scarlet cardigan and found Finlay's sister-in-law tidying up. On the bed lay a strange off-white sweater. 'Oh,' said Jessica, 'just what I need. Would anyone mind if I borrowed this?' It looked much heavier and more practical than her silly, skinny red cardigan. Finlay's sister-in-law smiled and Jessica took this for permission: she found nothing odd in the unexpected presence of the sweater. She'd needed one and there it was. Everything went dark as she pulled it over her head and when she emerged she blinked. Never again would she drink port. For a moment she had seen not Finlay's sister-in-law, not a woman, but something else, something you would definitely not expect to find in a bedroom. She blinked again and her vision returned to normal; the woman with her had assumed her usual, human form and was wiping over the dressing-table mirror in a natural everyday manner. Crikey, said Jessica to herself, wondering nervously about the properties of the port. Hooch, she thought: hallucinogenic hooch. My poor brain cells . . .

Jon walked round his room, thinking of Jessica, and then of someone else and then of Jessica again and he said aloud: 'Aah,' and then he wondered if he had been weeping and had forgotten, for his breath had caught as though on a sob. He heard the words 'Poor child' and looked round, but there was nobody there. 'Poor child,' he repeated and shook his head. A gust of wind rattled the window pane and the room was a room no longer, but the poop deck of a man-o'-war and he was no longer Jon but Errol Flynn and all the lovely women loved him. 'If you go to sea in that thin shirt, poor child,' he told himself, 'you'll be oh, so cold', and the sob rose again. There were some old sweaters in the wardrobe in the empty room at the end of the landing. He had seen them one night when he was on reconnaissance, when the cheating woman had locked her door against him and left him to roam the darkened corridors of a strange place all by himself. He went to the room quite openly as though he had every right, and took the top sweater. It smelled of tar and was cold to the touch, but when he pulled it on it warmed him and gave him courage so that he became a different person and laughed for joy.

There was no one there when he ran downstairs: no one to question or stop him, or even to tell him how handsome he looked in the seaman's sweater, but he didn't mind. Soon enough they would see what he could do and who he was — who he *really* was. Not Jon, not even Errol Flynn, but a hero like the men of myth, commanding the mighty waves single-handed, head erect, muscles taut while the merciless sea snarled and licked at the sides of his painted craft.

He had marked the craft a few days ago. It was tied to the end of the jetty where it bobbed invitingly up and down like another child saying: 'Play with me, play with me.'

'This is no game,' said Jon, sternly, as he struggled to untie the rope, all wet as it was and cramped against itself.

The tide was going out and like yet another child it implored: 'Come with me. Come with me.' As he freed the rope and jumped into the dinghy a squall lifted it high and then outwards on a retreating wave. 'We'll soon be under sail,' said Jon.

Eric, who was out in the front looking for the errant Finlay, watched disbelievingly as Jon began to make for America. 'Hi,' he yelled, pointlessly. He had seen him fiddling with the rope but it hadn't occurred to him that anyone but a lunatic would push off in a dinghy with no sail, no oars and a split in the seams. The bloody thing was half full of water already.

'Hi,' he yelled again. 'Come back.'

Another wave bore Jon further out.

'Sweet hell,' said Eric, looking round for Finlay. The wind returned with a sudden burden of rain and he could no longer see the dinghy. 'Finlay, where are you?' His voice faded to a moan and he fled into the inn.

'Ring the coastguard,' he shouted as he shot through to the back, and even as he spoke he wondered if he was over-reacting to what might be an insignificant event on this damned island. Maybe Jon knew what he was doing and had some unsuspected means of controlling the dinghy. Who knew what these sailing types might get up to. 'Finlay,' he screamed out in the inn yard, as he realized the unlikelihood of this.

'Why do we have to ring the coastguard?' asked Anita of Ronald who was finishing the cooling coffee. 'What's happened?'

'Where's Finlay?' screeched Eric as he flew in again. A drowning, more or less on the premises, wouldn't do trade any good at all.

'I don't know,' said Anita, rather put out at his lack of cere-mony.

'Then ring the coastguard,' howled Eric as he rushed out of the front door. *'Finlay.'*

'How does one ring the coastguard?' asked Anita. 'And why do we have to?' She followed Eric outside. 'What *is* going on?' she asked.

'The number's on the board by the phone,' said Jessica as Anita returned, unenlightened, since Eric had gone to the shore's edge and was hopping about in the rain waving his arms and shouting.

'I don't see why I should bother the coastguard when I don't know what's happening,' said Anita.

'He must have seen someone in trouble out there,' said Jessica, and she went herself to the phone in the hall and carefully dialled the number. The phone was dead.

'The phone's dead,' she said to Eric as he tore in, dripping. He snatched it off the hook and listened, then banged it down again.

Jessica wanted to say 'Told you so', but she didn't. She said: 'What's the matter?'

167

Eric, by now, had his hands in his hair. He stood still, trying to think. 'The professor,' he cried. 'The professor's got a dinghy. Come on.'

'Where are we going?' asked Ronald as they all automatically followed Eric's summons. The rain was coming down in sheets when they got to the door and visibility was what is known as 'limited'.

'Shit,' said Jessica. Ronald and Anita were putting on their coats with considered care but there was something in Eric's urgency which drew Jessica after him, and she grabbed the first garment to come to hand from the hall-stand. 'What *is* it?' she asked as they ran.

'It's that boy,' said Eric, gasping for breath. 'He's gone out in the inn dinghy and it's full of holes . . .' There was a figure walking towards them in the rain. 'Finlay?' shouted Eric.

'Harry,' said Jessica.

The professor's cottage door was closed against the weather and Eric hammered against it, still shouting.

'What's the panic?' asked the professor unwelcomingly, as he opened it, clad only in an insufficient towelling dressing-gown. Jessica took time to consider again her theory about men who habitually threw off their clothes, since he had obviously only just thrown on the gown and there were two girls in the kitchen. She determined to discuss it further with Harry.

'Can we use your phone?' said Eric.

'Why?' asked the professor.

'Because it's an emergency,' said Eric with commendable reserve since he wanted to shriek, *'Because it's an emergency, you mean, close-fisted bastard.'*

'I'll have to unlock it,' said the professor, reluctantly, and Eric put his hands in his hair again.

'What is it?' said Harry to Jessica.

'It's Jon,' said Jessica. 'He's gone out in a holey boat and Eric's trying to raise the coastguard.'

168

'This one's dead too,' wailed Eric when the phone had been made available to him. His voice cracked.

'Calm down,' said Harry. 'There's no time to wait for the coastguard anyway.'

'Then it's got to be his dinghy,' said Eric, pointing malevolently at the professor and daring him to refuse its use. 'Where is it?'

'It's pegged on the foreshore,' said the professor. 'But Finlay's borrowed the outboard-motor.'

'Then I'll have to row it,' said Eric.

'The tide's out,' said the professor, and Eric looked as though he might cry.

'It's all right,' said Harry. 'I'll drag it to the end of the causeway and launch it from there. The water's deep enough and it joins a channel . . .'

'You?' said Eric.

'I know this coast,' said Harry, and Jessica remembered that that deep water was where his boy had drowned.

'I'll come with you,' she said. 'I've done some sailing . . .' I sound like Jon, she thought.

'No,' said Harry. 'The dinghy won't take more than two and if . . .'

'If you have a return passenger,' said Jessica.

'Yes,' said Harry.

The causeway was hard and cold and wet; the world at its worst and most inimical. The rain its cruel collaborator, and the sea – the end.

'Don't go . . .' said Jessica, her shins bleeding from where she had fallen on the rock, her blood diluted in the salt rain. And then she said, 'You must take this,' and she took the old fur from her shoulders and passed it down to Harry in the bobbing dinghy, and she crouched in the seaweed, watching.

The rocks stretched out beyond her. She stared through the rain, half blinded, and saw shifting figures rising, and falling again, as though through a semi-opaque curtain, and she heard the wind. She saw a woman and a boy standing free of the sea. She saw their grey eyes. She saw the woman hold out her arms, and she saw the boy hold out his arms and Harry put the fur around him, and she said to herself, 'It is Jon, and Harry has saved him,' but then she looked again and as she saw a wave fall she saw the dinghy in its trough; saw someone clutch at its sides, fall back and clutch again, and then she saw it overturn and saw no more.

'Jessica,' someone was saying. 'Jessica, Jessica – are you all right?'

She opened her eyes. She had heard someone else speaking a minute ago; had heard Jon cry out in fear, and a woman saying, '. . . poor child. Don't be afraid.' Heard Harry saying, 'There is nothing to fear, nothing to fear at all.' Heard a younger voice saying, 'Father.' Heard Harry's voice again, changed by joy. Heard the music of a flute playing a tune so sweet and strange it might never have been heard on the earth before . . .

'Jessica,' she now heard faintly. 'Jessica, Jessica . . .'

'Bugger,' said Jessica and tried to sit up. Her head hurt.

'We thought you'd gone too,' said Eric hysterically. 'You were jumping round on the rock and you nearly went in.'

'I don't remember that,' said Jessica, putting her hand up.

'You've banged your head,' said Anita.

They were all there. All except Harry and Jon, and they had gone with the seal people to the edge of the world . . .

'What did you say?' asked Anita, kneeling beside her out of the wind.

'She's delirious,' said Eric. 'Is there a doctor in the house?' He felt delirious too. He looked from the psychoanalyst to the dentist as they stood uselessly by and watched. 'Don't either of you have any medical training?' he asked, not at all in the tone of a respectful innkeeper.

'It's only a graze,' said the professor.

'I'll examine her when we get her back to the hotel,' said

Ronald. It seemed much harder as they struggled back along the causeway. Probably, thought Jessica, because now there was no hurry. And no Harry . . .

'Don't cry,' said Anita in her new, nice voice.

'I'm not,' said Jessica.

Finlay was in the bar when they got back to the inn. He hadn't been there long, because he was quite as wet as any of them.

'Where the flaming hell were you?' asked Eric. He'd lost two guests. There'd be an inquiry. The bodies might never be washed up. There was a curse on the inn. Nobody would stay there ever again. Mabel would say it was all his own fault. Mabel might never come back. He wished he'd stayed in Telford. He wished he was dead, drowned and gone with his erstwhile clients.

'I had things to do,' said Finlay and, unbelievably, he blew a swift trill on his flute, and laughed.

'I'm packing it in,' said Eric that evening in the bar. 'I've had enough.' He had abandoned any attempt to keep the usual cordial yet respectful distance between an innkeeper and his guests. 'They don't want us here and I don't understand them. I'm off as soon as I can put this place on the market. What am I supposed to do now?' He had been to the police station and informed the policeman of the mishap and gained the impression that he would somehow be held responsible. 'I've *had* it,' said Eric.

'You can't be blamed,' said Anita, thereby implying that he could.

'Happens all the time,' said the professor. 'Treacherous coastline.'

'And what do I do with their things?' inquired Eric. 'Tell me that.'

'You send them back to their next of kin,' suggested Anita.

'Harry hadn't got any next of kin,' said Jessica, speaking for the first time that evening.

'Oh, great,' said Eric. 'And what about Jon? I guess he had none either?'

'No,' said Jessica. 'I don't think he did.' She could be helpful and ask her agent but she didn't want to. Her agent would be mildly annoyed with her for landing herself in trouble.

'So what do I do with the stuff?' Eric went on. 'I suppose I have to keep it here, shoved in drawers so there's no room for anything else.' He remembered all the old sweaters and furs he had had to dispose of. Half of them were still lying around somewhere.

'Get the police to take them away,' said Anita.

'I don't think they'd do that,' said Eric. 'I'll probably be accused of stealing them.'

'I have heard,' said Jessica, 'that drowning is rather pleasant. I have heard it said that when there is a fire on board the sailors take with delight to the water. I know it could be held that they have no option . . .'

'I don't see how it could be pleasant,' said Anita.

'I have heard,' continued Jessica, 'that being drowned induces a sense of euphoria. Although I don't see how anyone could really know.'

'I don't see that it matters,' said Anita.

'I don't suppose it does,' said Jessica.

'How's your head?' asked Anita.

Ronald had pronounced the injury superficial and Eric had put a plaster on it.

'It hurts,' said Jessica, but she smiled because Mrs H. had arrived and would find it more interestingly tragic if one of the morning's survivors was in great pain.

Mrs H. was thrilled to bits. A double drowning so close to home was even more exciting than the fouling of fishing-nets by trespassing submarines. 'What a terrible thing,' she said. 'What a dreadful thing to happen.' But now she was the one to be uniquely excluded from the company for she had not been on the causeway; not suffered the wind and the blinding rain and the feeble astonishment at seeing people with whom you had breakfasted being swept to destruction by a careless element. 'How did it happen?' she asked.

'Accident,' said Eric. 'The gale . . .' The wind had dropped, the sea was as still as a sleeping child and the air on the water as sweet as milk. Such an innocent world it seemed, now that it had eaten. Jessica put her hand to her head.

'What gale?' said Mrs H. 'There's been hardly a breath of wind all day.'

'You must be very sheltered up there,' said Eric. 'It's been blowing great guns down here.'

'It didn't say anything on the weather forecast,' said Mrs H.

'It never does,' said Eric unfairly.

'Sudden squall,' said the professor. 'Treacherous coastline.' He seemed obsessed by this anthropomorphic quality in the geography of the island, and Eric couldn't blame him. He thought on the whole it was quite an accurate summing-up. Wives and islands – thought Eric – each as untrustworthy as the other.

'Maybe it's the sea that brings down your fence,' suggested Mrs H., 'if it can get so rough down there.'

'I'd've noticed, wouldn't I?' said the professor. 'I'd've been bound to notice if the sea was in the garden.'

'Not if you weren't there,' said Mrs H.

'It happens when I *am* there,' said the professor. 'It happens all the time.'

Mrs H. could have kicked herself for bringing up the subject of his blasted fence: she wanted details of the day's catastrophe about which she was still vague.

'The dinghy's gone too,' said the professor.

'So's mine,' said Eric.

'Yours was knackered already,' said the professor. 'Finlay'd just finished working on mine.'

'*Finlay*,' said Eric. 'Finlay's a dead loss if you ask me. He's never around when you need him.' He did not care that Finlay's sister-in-law was behind him somewhere, and probably within earshot: he hoped she'd tell Finlay his candid opinion of him, although he suspected that Finlay would not be unduly discomposed at the hearing. 'Why wasn't he here with his damn boat?' he demanded. 'He could've prevented all this.'

'Finlay's boat's moored a couple of miles down the coast,' volunteered Mrs H. 'I saw it the other day.'

'What's it doing down there?' asked Eric. 'What's the use of that?' It was another instance of the maddening ways of the locals, irresponsible and inscrutable. They were just like the weather: the fiendish, carefree, murderous weather.

'I'd rather go back on the ferry,' said Anita.

'It looks as though you'll have to,' said Eric.

'Have you told their next of kin?' asked Mrs H., since no one seemed prepared to talk about what had happened.

'They haven't got any,' said Eric. 'Anyone want another drink?' Tonight he didn't care if he gave it away. All his hopes had been finally dashed, and now he was missing his wife unbearably. He knew perfectly well that if she came back she'd continue to make his life a misery, and he didn't care: she gave him moments that almost made up for it. He wouldn't care if she was rude to the Procurator Fiscal. It didn't seem to matter any more compared to the way she smiled when the weather was warm, basking on the inn wall where the boy had sat, laughing at the eel that Finlay had brought in a bucket and that had frightened Eric nearly to death.

'You all seem very casual about it,' said Mrs H. at last, petulantly.

'About what?' asked Eric.

'You know . . .' she said and gestured with her hands.

'We're all in shock,' claimed Anita.

'They have not yet had time . . .' said Ronald, electing now to exclude himself from the rest, '. . . to fully appreciate the nuances and repercussions of what has happened today. A sudden, unexpected and traumatic event such as they witnessed this morning will require time and possibly informed assistance before they will be able fully to assimilate and hopefully to come to terms with it. In some cases they may feel a residual sense of guilt at either what they perceive as a lack of due preparation for one of the major circumstances of existence, or a failure to preclude and forestall it. It is not impossible that some may feel they should have offered further endeavours to prevent what they consider an accidental occurrence. They are not however . . .' he continued, '. . . in shock. Shock is a pathological state typified by hypothermia, a swift and shallow pulse rate . . .'

'Oh, do shut up,' said Anita. He had hardly said a word to her all day, had said nothing to indicate that they would go on meeting when they returned to London and now he had contradicted her.

'What gets me,' said Eric, who had been brooding, 'is that I could have sworn there was someone else on the causeway. You couldn't see properly but for a minute I thought a fishing boat must have come up. I could have sworn I saw that boy who goes past here most days, but I can't have done because even if they'd tried to help and failed they wouldn't have gone away without saying something, would they? I didn't see a boat go out either, did you?' he appealed to the others.

'It was probably the seals you saw,' said the professor. 'There're dozens of them about.'

'I guess it must have been,' said Eric. 'But it looked like people.'

'In those conditions,' said the professor, 'you couldn't have seen an ocean liner properly. I could hardly see a damn thing.' He was already beginning to feel guilty and make excuses for himself, noted Ronald with impartial satisfaction.

'I'm going to bed,' said Jessica. She had made up her mind

175

to take Harry's book about General Gordon home with her. She knew nothing about publishing but her agent would doubtless know somebody who did. If he hadn't quite finished it, she'd finish it herself.

His door was unlocked, the room scrupulously tidy: a hypocritically gentle breeze lifted the curtain by the window and Jessica shivered. She opened the wardrobe and looked steadfastly at his clothes. It was absurd that a person's clothes should remain when he had gone. What did they think they were doing, just hanging there? The MS lay on the small table where Harry had worked. She picked it up and put a rubber-band round it, then she opened the table drawer and looked inside. It held a framed photograph of a woman and a boy, standing with their backs to the sea: she recognized them immediately, for had she not seen them only that morning? She took it and put it in the bottom of her suitcase and she never showed it to another living soul.

Downstairs, Eric looked round at his reduced clientele: they seemed to be settling in for the night, hunched over brimming glasses, telling tales of disaster in low voices.

'I had a friend whose aunt was drowned,' said Anita. 'In the Serpentine.'

'I didn't think you could drown in the Serpentine,' said Mrs H.

'You can drown in the bath,' said the professor. 'You could drown in a puddle if you kept your face down.'

'Why would anyone want to?' asked Anita. 'My friend's aunt fell out of a boat and she was dead when they got to her.'

'Perhaps she had a heart attack,' said the professor.

'She drowned,' said Anita. 'They did an autopsy and she'd drowned.'

'How did she fall in?' asked Mrs H.

'I don't know the details,' said Anita. 'My friend was too upset to tell me.'

Eric wanted to go to bed for he felt exhausted by the events of the day. It was all right for them: they didn't have to do anything but sit around gossiping about the deaths of strangers. He'd asked Finlay's sister-in-law to stay late but it seemed she had better things to do. Knowing that a whisky would not help to wake him up he nevertheless gave himself a double: after several of those he might get his second wind, for it didn't look as though he was going to get an early night. Anita was sitting beside Ronald in the manner of a wife, knees together, unsmiling though not disapproving and prepared to be silent should Ronald show signs of wishing to speak. Eric could have kicked her. Looking back he realized he had found it soothing to have the inn full of single people with no loving couples to rouse his envy and exacerbate his unhappiness. If Mabel had been different he could have looked kindly on breeding pairs, but as it was they made him sick. He wished he could stop thinking about his wife. *Wife*, he thought. Some wife to leave a man on his own to run a hotel with no help but a drunken boatman and a weird woman who danced off into the night whenever he needed her. As he glowered at Anita he thought that Mabel had never sat beside him like that, had never waited for him to speak, nor kept her knees together. She had lounged around with her limbs carelessly disposed for anyone to see, and she had laughed at whatever pleased her without ever referring to him for approval or permission. She had never even pretended to belong to him and when he had — no matter how covertly — assumed ownership of her she had flown into one of her rages, white with fury and leaping out of his reach with the slippery strength of a great fish. He was undoubtedly better off without her and he missed her until he thought his heart would break. Coldly he told himself that this misery was reaction to the dreadful events of the day: he had not — as Ronald would put it — assimilated the full meaning and made the appropriate adjustment. In a day or two he would be himself again and able to make rational decisions. At the back of his mind there lurked the awareness that he would not find it easy to sell the inn, and the only decision open to him was to knuckle down and make the best of it – without his wife. He was appalled to find himself weeping and hastened out of the bar to the inn yard where he stood in the cold taking deep breaths. From down the coast in the direction of the professor's cottage came the sound of music: the locals were up to their tricks again. He listened for a while, half outraged that they could make merry when two people had drowned and half meanly gratified that they were probably making a shocking mess of the professor's lawn: he wondered vaguely who they were; then suddenly curiosity got the better of him. To his own mild astonishment he took off his shoes, crossed the narrow road and walked along the shore to spy on the illicit dancers, the tears drying on his chilled cheeks, the moon lighting his way.

To the end of his days Eric couldn't make up his mind whether or not he wished he hadn't done that. To the end of his days he couldn't make up his mind whether he had seen what he thought he saw or whether he had gone momentarily insane. The dead do not return to dance at the scene of their demise: that could not have been Harry with a woman and the boy with the fishing rod who had so often passed the inn on the way to the sea. Nor could that have been Jon sitting in the ruins of the professor's fence and laughing.

Eric had stood barefoot on the ice-cold sand, rubbing his eyes and trying to shout to Finlay, who was capering about with his flute, but he seemed to have lost his voice as you lose your voice in dreams. The music was so sweet: it crept over his consciousness as the soft summer tide creeps over the shore, and Eric thought he was fainting. He threw back his head for the wind to clear it, but the wind had dropped and the music grew louder, the dance wilder. There were others there whom he recognized and many who were strange to him: he had not known the island contained so many people . . . the moon went behind a cloud, something brushed past him and he staggered, somebody laughed again and he could smell seaweed, intensely strong. 'Watch out,' thought Eric, but no words came. Nervous breakdown, he thought. I'm having a nervous breakdown and I'm not surprised.

'It's getting beyond a joke,' said a voice and Eric blinked as the lights in the cottage came on, illuminating the flattened lawn. 'I'll have the law on the bastards,' continued the professor, 'or I'll get a shotgun and sit up all night until I catch them at it. I'll . . .'

'Oh, let's get inside and close the doors,' cried his girls. 'What does it matter?'

'What do you mean – what does it matter?' inquired the irate householder. 'It's taking liberties. It's illegal. It's trespassing and criminal damage . . .'

'It's cold,' wailed the girls.

Eric couldn't move: he stood on the sand like a rock.

'Who's there?' yelled the professor, catching sight of him. 'Come here you . . .'

'It's me,' said Eric, finding his voice at last. There was no one in the garden now. No one, that is, but the maddened professor, for the girls had gone inside.

'What the hell are you doing there?' asked this person, leaping to conclusions.

'It wasn't me,' said Eric, alerted to the professor's suspicions by his tone. 'I mean I didn't push over your fence.'

'Then what are you doing there?' asked the professor, not unreasonably.

'I thought I heard noises,' said Eric.

'Then why didn't you tell me?' said the professor. 'We might have caught them.'

'I wasn't sure,' lied Eric, whose principal concern was that the professor shouldn't notice that he had no shoes on. It seemed somehow vitally important.

179

'Well, did you see anyone?' demanded the professor, and there was a long pause.

'No,' said Eric eventually, and the professor stamped his foot on the sea-soaked earth.

'They're animals,' he said. 'Quite apart from the damage they do, how can they carry on like that after what happened this morning?'

But Eric didn't agree with him. He had a strong sense that it was not the dancers but the professor who was the interloper here. His perceptions had altered during the dance. He wondered how he would discuss the day-to-day running of the inn with Finlay's sister-in-law when last he had seen her she was dancing with the dead.

Jessica upset the ladder fern in the morning. She didn't mean to, not consciously. She was standing looking out of the dining-room window for she knew not what, and when she saw nothing, either expected or unexpected, she turned away and over went the fern with a crash of brass bowl.

'Don't cry,' said Anita, when she'd recovered from the fright.

'*I'm not*,' said Jessica, breathing deeply, her shoes full of spilled earth. Now Harry had gone she had no one to talk to, and she couldn't remember when she had felt more cruelly deprived.

'It's the reaction,' said Anita, passing her a tissue from her handbag.

'It'll be all right,' said Eric, plying dust-pan and brush and wondering what was likely to happen next. 'I'll just repot it.'

'I'm sorry,' said Jessica. 'I'm hopelessly clumsy sometimes.' She took off a shoe and emptied the earth into the dust-pan, still snivelling a little.

'I might not even bother,' said Eric, picking up the fern by what would have been its scruff if it had been an animal. Jessica thought it was ironic that Jon had imagined her to be such a plant lover when the principal feeling a growing thing had inspired in her was acute dislike. She shook out the other shoe.

'What's the time?' she asked. Now she couldn't wait to leave the island.

'You may have to come back for the inquest, you know,' said Eric, dropping the fern carelessly into the pot.

This had not previously occurred to Jessica. 'All of us?' she demanded.

'I don't know,' said Eric. 'I don't know the form.'

'I may not be able to,' she said. 'Not if I'm in rehearsal.'

'I think you may have to,' said Eric.

'Like an enchantment,' said Jessica, thinking of those places – usually islands – which laid a spell on people so that they could never stay away.

'The law,' said Eric. 'You can't mess about with the law.'

'No,' said Jessica, accepting this prosaic proposal. 'I suppose you can't.' She went upstairs and threw things into her suitcase. The sweater she left on the bed.

'I've left the sweater on the bed,' she said to Eric as he came to help her carry the case down.

'You can keep it if you like,' said Eric indifferently, but Jessica didn't think she'd need it again. She had too many clothes already. Finlay's sister-in-law passed on her way to strip the beds and tidy everything away and Jessica thanked her for looking after them so nicely. The woman smiled and spoke the first words Jessica had heard her utter.

'Ye'll be back,' she said.

Jessica gave Ronald and Anita the slip on Glasgow station. She didn't want to see them any more. All the way home she read *The Tenant of Wildfell Hall* – indeed she reread much of it since her attention kept wandering. She enjoyed the bit where Helen tells Lady Lowborough to get lost, although she wouldn't have liked to have to say the lines on stage:

'... because it is painful to be always disguising my true sentiments respecting you, and straining to keep up an appearance of civility and respect towards one for whom I have not the most distant shadow of esteem...' Difficult, that, thought Jessica, muttering the words under her breath and thinking that if Harry hadn't drowned she could have tried out the passage on him. As it was the lady across the aisle obviously found her eccentric. Jessica realized she was wearing an inappropriate expression for a solitary passenger: she had adopted a high and haughty look and was peering down her nose in the effort to resemble Helen Huntingdon. For the time being she found it easier to play Helen than to be herself. Then she took up Harry's MS. She thought the beginning particularly good. She flicked through the rest and when she turned to the last page she saw that he had written 'The End'. She was glad to be relieved of the necessity of finishing it herself for she would not have been able to. Harry and General Gordon began to seem to her to be one and the same person. Somehow this also made everything easier.

Anita guided Ronald to an empty section of the train: she would have looked to an imaginative observer like a small animal bossing a larger in the manner of a corgi with a cow, which inevitably made Ronald look slightly stupid. She had determined to bring matters between them to a head and to this end had washed her hair in the small hours of the morning, which meant that she was now feeling unusually weary. 'I'm dreadfully tired,' she said plaintively, but Ronald did not respond: he seemed not to be noticing her shining hair.

Anita changed tack and surreptitiously ingested one of her vitamin pills. 'I feel better now,' she said, after a mile or two. 'I think I'm getting over the shock. Things like that have much more effect on one than one realizes.'

'Mmph,' said Ronald, who was thinking about his cold, empty house and the patients who would be neurotically annoyed with him for going on holiday: he considered them selfish and thoughtless and was growing increasingly uninterested in their boring problems. Where should he have his supper this evening? What would he do tomorrow?

'What did you feel when you saw them go down?' asked Anita, thinking that an intimate question such as this must lead to a discussion which would bring them closer, but Ronald was now thinking about Krafft-Ebing and sadomasochism and asking himself whether anything made sense. '*Ronald,*' insisted Anita.

'What?' he said.

'When they went down,' said Anita, who on reflection was finding her question rather foolish. 'What did you feel?'

'Who?' said Ronald, trying to wrench himself back to the present. Anita regarded him with disbelief: he seemed to have forgotten already that two people had drowned in his vicinity. She couldn't be expected to understand that he was accustomed to horror by listening daily to tales – imaginary or not – of dark events and undigested tragedy.

'Harry and Jon,' she reminded him.

'I thought someone should get them out,' said Ronald, indifferently.

'They tried,' said Anita. 'We *all* went as near to the edge as we could, but it was too late.'

'Yes,' said Ronald, 'so there was nothing to be done.'

This was undeniable but Anita still found his attitude perplexing. It was inhuman – not so much because he seemed not to care as because he seemed incurious. Perhaps, she told herself, it was his profession which had distanced him from the human race and that he was, in fact, a superior type of person in his very impartiality.

'What time do you suppose they serve lunch?' he asked.

Anita longed to rebuke him for worrying about food at a time like this, but she dared not. He seemed a different man from the one she had walked and talked with on the island and she feared he was slipping away from her as Harry and Jon . . . She thought she might cry in a minute and she had a despairing sense that Ronald wouldn't notice. Everything was going wrong. It was like a shipboard romance, she thought miserably, and she didn't know what to do to retrieve the situation. It looked as though she'd be going back to the department after all. Nothing had really changed. 'I haven't given you my telephone number,' she said, and she wrote it down on the back of an envelope and passed it to him.

He looked at it with apparent incomprehension and put it in his breast pocket. It would go to the drycleaner's, reflected Anita, and never be seen again.

Jessica avoided Ronald and Anita when they got to Euston and sneaked into a taxi. Anita stood alone as Ronald said, 'Excuse me a moment,' and disappeared in the direction of Platform 2. He had seen a woman who resembled his wife.

Finlay was heading towards the island, back to Turncoat Inn, under a heavy rain. Mabel sat in the cabin wearing a new fur and looking quite cheerful. If her husband asked where she'd got it from she'd say she'd got it dirt-cheap from a place where the animal-rights protesters had moved in.

'Got a light?' she called, sticking her head out in time to observe Finlay waving to three seals who were passing in the opposite direction. 'You're nuts,' she said, 'you're all nuts.' She cupped her hands about the match to shield it from the wind and the rain, and the light glowed through the transparency of her webbed fingers. 'Ugh,' she said, 'bloody weather . . . I must be nuts too, coming back.'

'Och,' said Finlay, 'ye all come back in the end.'

Afterword

Rereading this sparkling novel about an island at the edge of the world, I'm reminded of the time when I found the author herself on an island in the middle of nowhere.

Desert Island Discs is a venerable British radio interview program which each week asks a renowned guest to play along with the idea that he or she is exiled on a desert island. The premise gives the familiar question-and-answer format an often entertaining twist. How would the "castaway" cope? Which half-dozen or so recordings would make up the castaway's desert island music library? (Choosing the discs, listening to bits of them, and explaining why they were chosen are of course the signature elements of the show.) In addition to the Bible and the works of Shakespeare, sturdy copies of which are island fixtures, what other book would the castaway hope to find washed ashore? What "luxury" item would supplement the bare necessities? Indeed what "necessity" would be considered most necessary of all? And again, just how *would* the castaway cope?

Very well, thank you, was Alice Thomas Ellis's response. Some plainsong, some Billie Holiday, the haunting basso of Paul Robeson, the witty malice of Tom Lehrer's "Poisoning Pigeons in the Park," and for luxury "a comfortable sofa" — certainly those items would ease the rigors of her solitude, but plainly it was Alice Thomas Ellis's attitude that exile on a desert island was rather something to look forward to than dread. Her interviewer called attention to Ellis's having in her youth been a postulant in a convent: mustn't that have been something like being on a desert island? Something like, yes. Well, then, if that was the sort of life she wanted why had she left? And as Ellis's lovely voice offered poised

185

and witty rejoinders to the increasingly cranky questions it became clear that this castaway's calm and essentially welcoming acceptance of her desert islanding was getting quite under the skin of her interrogator. You weren't supposed to *want* to be there; the fun lay in emphasizing just how unendurable it all would be. Surely one's "island mentality" would be characterized by frustration and fear and a junkie's itch for another big fix of civilization, blessed civilization?

Not so, in Alice Thomas Ellis's case; and perhaps had the interviewer been more deeply familiar with her castaway's books she might instead have called attention to the fact that being a castaway is precisely the condition which defines the human soul throughout Ellis's work. As castaways from divine grace, there isn't much (and maybe in fact there is absolutely nothing) that men and women can do finally to save themselves but wait, islanded, in faith – a belief subtly touched on in this novel when Harry quotes General Gordon's striking and memorable words from Khartoum: "Nothing can be more abject and miserable than the usual conception of God. Accept what I say – namely that He has put us in a painful position (I believe with our perfect consent, for if Christ came to do His will, so did we, His members) to learn what He is, and that He will extricate us."

Few in Ellis's books adhere to such a belief; most just keep wrongheadedly trying to do it themselves – DIY salvation – and their antics are frequently the source of the acerbic comedy in Ellis's novels. In *The Inn at the Edge of the World*, for instance, a handful of miserable urbanites suppose that by fleeing to what amounts to the "next-best-thing to a desert island" they can each escape the unhappiness which in their respective fashions they have all come to label "Christmas." But their miseries, like their suitcases, are lugged with them; their escapes, like all such temporal shiftings, are only into other confinement. "They change the

186

sky, but not their minds, who sail across the sea" – their being who they are rules out their finding what they profess to be in search of. And when confronted on the island by evidences of the uncanny, all they can do is blunder after explanations founded only in their everyday reason, dooming themselves to an unenlightened return to things as they were and as they will most decidedly remain. Serves them, I suspect the author feels, right ("There is nothing more infuriating than resolute rationality in the face of the inexplicable").

But consider, by way of contrast, the "island mentality" whose existence is announced in the novel's opening words. In simplest terms, one can say that what characterizes that mentality is its embrace of – its complicity with – the uncanny. On the island there is simply another order of reality than can be tidily accounted for by interlopers like Eric and his Christmas escapees. ("You've never seen an electric current but you believe in them, don't you?") As in many of her novels, the supernatural fable which Ellis weaves allows her, I believe, to speak as in parable of the uncanniness of the divine. To draw the analogy point by point would be tedious and unhelpful, but on my reading the analogy is there to be drawn.

So had I been in that interviewer's chair, briefly sharing the desert island air with Alice Thomas Ellis, I would have tried to steer the conversation quickly round to the shrewd tale which I hope you've just read and thoroughly enjoyed. To explore, on an island of the mind, island mentalities with this inspired writer might have made, I imagine, for conversation worth attending to.

Thomas Meagher
Editorial Director, A COMMON READER

About The Author

ALICE THOMAS ELLIS is one of England's most widely admired writers. Her fiction includes *The Sin Eater* (1977), which received a Welsh Arts Council Award for a "book of exceptional merit"; *The 27th Kingdom* (1982), which was nominated for a Booker Prize; and *The Inn at the Edge of the World* (1990), which won the 1991 Writers' Guild Award for Best Fiction. Her most recent novel is *Fairy Tale* (1996). Alice Thomas Ellis has five children and lives in London and Wales.